A Grand Night
for Murder

A GRAND NIGHT
FOR MURDER

H. PAUL JEFFERS

St. Martin's Press

New York

Production Editor: David Stanford Burr

Library of Congress Cataloging-in-Publication Data

Jeffers, H. Paul (Harry Paul).
    A grand night for murder / H. Paul Jeffers.
        p.   cm.
    ISBN 0-312-13084-8
    I. Title.
PS3560.E36G7   1995
813'.54–dc20   95-15231
                                                            CIP

First Edition: July 1995

10   9   8   7   6   5   4   3   2   1

For Sid,
for the Saturday dinners

The detective story is the normal recreation of noble minds.

—PHILIP GUEDALLA

A GRAND NIGHT
FOR MURDER

Dressed to Kill

IN THE SPIRIT of the invitations that dinner guests should "dress to kill," Prudence Westmoreland had bought a bloodred gown.

As planner of the festivities, she arrived at the hotel an hour early and went directly across the lobby to make sure the "events" signboard was correct. It read:

MYSTERY WRITERS OF AMERICA
EDGAR ALLAN POE AWARDS
GRAND BALLROOM
6:30 P.M.

Satisfied, she proceeded to a gracefully curving staircase and ascended to the second-floor ballroom. Immediately within, she found two long baize-covered tables stacked with copies of the program. Its slick cover was in black, white, and red, and featured a glowering sketch of the inventor of the detective story. Inside were pages of articles by officers of the MWA and essays from four past recipients of the world of mystery's version of the Motion Picture Academy's Oscar and TV's Emmy. A small porcelain bust of Poe, it was familiarly known as the Edgar.

Many pages of advertisements by book publishers acclaimed and congratulated their own authors who had been nominated for the coveted trophy in the categories of best novel of the year, best first novel, best fact crime, best short story, best paperback, best critical/biographical study or autobiography, and best juvenile novel. Other ads hailed nominees for the best motion picture, best television feature, and best series.

Looking across the ballroom, she observed a dozen black-jacketed waiters also making last-minute checks of arrangements, flitting like bats amid a sea of large round tables each set for ten. Draped in crisp white covers and laid with blue china and glittering silver and glassware, each had been graced by a floral centerpiece with a little flagpole jutting upward to display a numbered card. To find one's place, a guest looked to the alphabetical listing in the program and noted his or her table number, an arrangement that made for interesting conversations by frequently situating a well-established author next to an associate member still striving to be published. Further tables had been reserved by publishers with Edgar-nominated authors on their lists, literary agents, and others in the trade of literary criminality discerning benefit through their presence.

Table One was reserved for MWA elected officers and the person whose name was to be endowed with the title "Grand Master," which counted an illustrious roster of recipients, starting with Agatha Christie. It included, among others, Eric Ambler, James M. Cain, John Dickson Carr, Dorothy Salisbury Davis, Erle Stanley Gardner, Graham Greene, Ed McBain, Ngaio Marsh, collaborators Frederic Dannay and Manfred B. Lee (known as Ellery Queen), Rex Stout, and Julian Symons.

Adjacent to the head table stood a podium flanked by a pair of tables. On these the Edgar statuettes, second-place plaques, and framed certificates for the runners-up had been laid out in order of presentation. Covering them from any inquisitive and impatient eyes, white sheets suggested shrouded corpses.

The final award to be handed out was not a secret. But the choice of Jonathan Dodge as Grand Master was controversial. It had been approved by the awards committee at the close of a stormy meeting by a majority of one. Outraged, the chairman had threatened to resign.

"That dreadful creature?" Myron Frank had thundered. "Over my dead body."

Previous Grand Master recipient Elvira Eveland had exhibited her usual macabre sense of humor. "You're not alone in not loving Jonathan," she had declared. "But, really Myron, why should it be over *your* dead body? How about *his?*"

PART ONE

The Countryside

It is my belief, Watson, founded upon my experience, that the lowest and vilest alleys in London do not present a more dreadful record of sin than does the smiling and beautiful countryside.

—SHERLOCK HOLMES

Traitor's Lair

"YOU BETTER COME QUICK, Mr. G," the workman blared as he barged into the library. "There's a dead man in the boathouse."

Lifting his eyes from his word processor, Morgan Griffith picked up a favorite pipe. Inserting a fingertip in the bowl to tamp the tobacco, he found it had gone out. Wiping the smudged finger on his blue sweater, he realized he had forgotten about the bent black briar as he scrolled through a story of deception, betrayal, and murder that would become an obsession for a sleuth as relentless as every fictional detective who had come deducing down the literary pike. Turning in an antique swivel chair with a cane seat that squeaked nicely, he said, "Mr. Fulmer, I think if you look more closely you will find it's an animal carcass."

"There's no mistake," Fulmer replied breathlessly. Fingers gnarled during three decades of laboring for transplanted city folk twirled a baseball cap. "This corpse is wearin' a tuxedo."

Griffith tapped the "save" button. "All right. Show me."

"Best put galoshes on," Fulmer said as Griffith rose. "It's really muddy down there, on account of the rain."

Winter had been hard. The snow had been relentless, six storms in as many weeks with temperatures barely above zero. But with springtime under way in earnest, Griffith had hired Fulmer to demolish the boathouse and the eyesores of a collapsing stable, a half-burned barn, and the crumbling stone ruins of an even more ancient icehouse. That done, a culling of several trees and wildly rampant underbrush would follow. By summer he hoped to enjoy a spectacular unobstructed view from the house of the magnificent river and, on the distant opposite shoreline, the melancholy walls of Sing Sing Prison.

What once upon a time had been the boathouse had rotted to a dilapidated pile of wooden walls barely supporting a perilously sagging roof. Of equal precariousness was a rickety roofed jetty which had berthed the yacht of the original owner of the rustic site about an hour's drive from New York City. A theatrical and motion picture star of the first magnitude in the silent era, Ilona Troy had spearheaded a 1930s invasion of idyllic Stone County by the rich and celebrated New Yorkers who had weathered the Wall Street crash unscathed. Taking Troy's cue, they scooped up riverfront properties at bargain prices to create summertime havens for themselves. Three decades later, the properties had been sold again, this time by heirs intent upon reaping fortunes through subdivision of the estates to accommodate a flood of latter-day refugees from the teeming metropolis downriver.

Only Troy had held fast, becoming more and more reclusive as her beautiful house and land drifted into decay and her finances into bankruptcy, until she was found dead before a massive fireplace in the library of the large white house. Dated by the Stone County Historical Society to the Revolutionary War, it was said to have been occupied for a few days by the British spy Major André while he conspired with Benedict Arnold for the surrender of nearby West Point. Tradition had bestowed upon it a name that would prove to be irresistible to Griffith: Traitor's Lair.

The author of five espionage thrillers and seventeen hard-boiled detective novels, he had purchased it from the actress's sole heir three months before.

About a hundred yards from the house the ruin toward which the two men rushed slanted slightly to the left at the bottom of a sloping lawn overgrown during years of inattention. The black river lapped at pilings beneath wooden stairs that gave way a little as Griffith ascended them. When his eyes adjusted to the darkness within, he found weak light seeping through the narrow spaces in slatted walls. Amazingly, very little of the rain of Friday night and Saturday had trickled through the roof. Forming long thin fingers, the meager light striped a portly middle-aged, gray-haired figure reposing immediately inside the door, as if the body had been laid out for a funeral. The striking of a match turned the pale face with its open, staring eyes and gaping mouth into an eerie mask.

"Do you have any idea who he is, sir?" Fulmer whispered.

"It's Jonathan Dodge. I saw him at the Edgars Friday night."

2

Benson's Bailiwick

"I HOPE I DIDN'T WAKE YOU."

Stone County District Attorney Aaron Benson's youthful voice came through Arlene Flynn's phone with the same gentlemanly tone which had persuaded juries to return guilty verdicts in every one of his murder cases. Of more than a hundred, seventeen had been tried and won during her six years as his chief investigator.

"Just having breakfast and plodding through the newspapers on a lazy, gray Sunday. What's up?"

"The sheriff's office just phoned. Deputy Blake is up at the old Troy estate. He thinks we might have a homicide. Can you put on your boots and be ready in ten minutes?"

In six years of countless such summonses she had never kept him waiting for her to dress. Donning sensible shoes and slacks immediately upon arising, even on weekends, had become as natural to her as the weight of the .38-caliber police special revolver she carried in a handbag. This morning she placed it in one of tan leather that complemented beige trousers, a brown and white houndstooth jacket, and brown hiking boots. As she strode from the snug split-level ranch-style house with five minutes to spare before the blue sedan which Stone County afforded its prosecutor drew up, a damp breeze teased her short auburn hair.

Though the handsome, slender man at its wheel was forty-five, newspaper stories about him invariably described him as "boyish." Flynn could not argue with the adjective.

Since the day she went to work for him he appeared not to have aged an hour, whereas she always seemed to find strands of gray infringing her reddish hair and crowsfeet lines at the corners of eyes that had been described twenty years earlier in her high school class yearbook as being "as smilingly and beguilingly Irish as her name." The annual had also listed her most likely to become a movie star in roles for which Maureen O'Hara had grown too mature.

That she chose to attend the John Jay College of Criminal Justice in New York City to become a cop had been the talk of her first class reunion. By the tenth-year gathering, she had earned the golden shield of detective third class of the New York Police Department. At the twentieth, no one had to be told that she had become D.A. Aaron Benson's chief investigator. By then she had helped convict three murderers.

"What makes Freddy Blake think it's a homicide?" she asked as she slid into the passenger seat, carefully placing her feet out of the way of police scanners, telephones, and radios crowded under the dashboard.

"He said, 'Something's really fishy about this.'"

"Well, I've never known Freddy's nostrils to go wrong."

"I've ordered up a crime scene team from the state police and told Freddy to secure the area. Thankfully, the location is so far in the sticks there's no risk that crowds of the morbidly curious will descend to screw it up. Besides Blake, the only people at the scene are the new owner of Traitor's Lair and the workman who actually found the body in an old abandoned boathouse on the property."

"I'm familiar with it. Some of us kids used to explore it when we went out hiking."

Twenty minutes later, as the car swung from the blacktop road into a driveway all but obscured by thick shrubs and low-hanging limbs of shading trees, Benson said, "What a spooky place."

"This used to be a lovers lane," Flynn replied.

Benson gave her an amused glance. "How do you know?"

She smiled coquettishly. *"I'll* never tell."

Presently, they emerged into sunlight and onto a macadam parking area adjacent to a weathered fieldstone house. Blake was leaning against the trunk of a white sheriff's patrol car, next to a ramshackle old yellow station wagon and a gleaming new black four-wheel-drive minivan. Raising his right hand to the flat brim of his round brown hat, the deputy snapped a salute.

"This is as close as we can get with a vehicle," he said as the district attorney stepped from his car. "The way to the boathouse is pretty slippery. I almost fell on my butt a couple of times, so watch your step."

Ground that had been frozen solid in the winter now felt spongy and made wet sucking sounds with the lifting of each foot. Though it had been trodden by numerous feet before hers, Flynn did her best to confine her brown rubber-soled boots to Blake's huge imprints. Some of the other tracks, she presumed, had been left by the two men watching their progress from a porch at the rear of the house. Four worn plank steps leading to a slightly opened door bore the mud left by three different pairs of shoes, again presumably those of the two men and Blake. Choosing not to add to them, she asked him, "Where's the body?"

"Flat on its back just inside the door. He's lying there like he was asleep. Arms at his sides. All spiffed up in a monkey suit like a headwaiter in some fancy restaurant. I'd say the body hasn't been there very long, on account of there's no odor. It doesn't look as if there was time for animals to get at it."

"An excellent observation, Freddy," Benson said. "Why did you think it might be a homicide?"

"On account of there not being a weapon that I could see. And nothing points to it being suicide. I figure, if you're going to kill yourself in a place like this, you throw a rope over a beam. Or use a gun. I didn't see either. Plus the fact that the owner of the property said he didn't hear a shot and he had no idea that this Jonathan Dodge was even around the place. That's the dead man's name. Jonathan Dodge. He's an old friend of the owner, Morgan Griffith. He's a writer from the city. He bought the place a couple of months ago. The one who discovered the body is a local contractor, name of Jeb Fulmer, that Griffith hired to rip down this shack. Everything just looked fishy to me."

"Whatever happened here," said the district attorney, "the forensic boys and the coroner will sort it out."

For Flynn, the next few minutes became a mix of the strange and the familiar. Though the location of the investigation was new, she recognized every person who trudged down the hill. To the boathouse trooped experts in the implements of death: a photographer to record anything holding promise of an answer, fingerprint seekers and other stern-visaged, white-gloved men and women accustomed to poking around and probing the detritus of the unexplained, and therefore suspicious, death of a human being.

Entering the boathouse, she found the interior ablaze with the light of battery-powered lamps, which cast long, distorted, and ghostlike shadows of the crime scene team against rotting walls and across age-dried floorboards thick with the dust of decades. At the focus of the light lay the body, incongruously neat in tuxedo, black tie, immaculate stiff white shirt with a row of gold and diamond studs down the front, and matching cuff links.

Hunkering down, she pointed to the gleaming black patent leather shoes and asked of no one in particular, "He certainly didn't get in here on his own two feet, did he?"

"I see what you mean," murmured Benson, bending beside her. "There's no mud on the soles. The same goes for the bottom of the pants. It wasn't robbery. Look at those stones. A Rolex watch."

"You're in good shape, boss. You work out every day. Could you carry a man that size by yourself? Dead weight, too."

"Probably not. But I know some guys who could. Once you got him up on your shoulders, he could be handled."

"Downhill and in the mud that's out there? And at night?"

"He could have been dumped here during the day."

"Night's more likely, I think."

Benson came up straight. "Do you see any wounds? Any blood on him? I don't."

"There's no evident bruising. But there could be under his clothing."

Presently, the medical examiner of Stone County would come to examine and ponder and, if they were lucky, offer an immediate opinion as to the cause of death. Much more likely, however, his verdict would be held in abeyance while the corpse was carted to the place that Dr. Theodore Zeligman described as a world in which death delighted to help the living.

Like the district attorney, the coroner was dressed more suitably for an office than the muck and mud of a riverbank. Benson's three-button gray plaid with vest was fashionable. Dr. Zeligman's double-breasted navy blue appeared to date from World War II. Out of breath from negotiating the slippery descent, he was eight years past an age when most men of his generation, with much less demanding jobs, put away their suits and ties and put in for pensions. In thirty-five years as Stone County's medical examiner and during a decade as assistant coroner, he had determined the causes of thousands of deaths in the city morgues.

With a nod and a wave at Benson and Flynn as he entered, he went directly to the body. "May I begin?" he asked of those in the boathouse. "Has everybody done what has to be done in here?"

"He's all yours, Ted," Benson answered. "We'll be outside."

Emerging ten minutes later, Zeligman declared, "It's a very *tidy* corpse. Quite unlikely he died of a natural cause."

"If he'd just dropped dead," Flynn said with a tug at her pouty lower lip, "he wouldn't have gone down quite so neatly."

"So the body was placed there?" asked the district attorney.

"The autopsy will tell us for sure," Zeligman answered.

"How soon can we know?" asked Flynn.

Zeligman smiled. "Not soon enough to satisfy you, I'm sure, my dear. Tomorrow. Maybe. Have you identified him, Aaron?"

"The owner of the property says his name is Jonathan Dodge."

The coroner let out a little whistle. "The author?" He laid a consoling hand on Benson's shoulder. "Well, well, my friend, it appears you've got a headline-maker in your bailiwick."

Flynn turned aside. "I'll start with a chat with the owner of the place."

3

The Empty House

SHIELDING THE BOWL of his pipe from the wind with the cup of his left hand, Griffith held a match to it with his right. "Shall I assume," he asked as a gust whipped and snuffed out the flame, "that I'm a suspect in this murder?"

Flynn's eyes went wide. "Why do you suppose it's murder?"

Griffith tucked the pipe into a pocket of his blue sweater. "He didn't just lie down and die in that shack, did he?"

"Why not suicide?"

Griffith snorted. "Jonathan Dodge would never kill himself. His ego wouldn't permit, especially while he was working on a new book. Not with another of his best-sellers about to hit the bookstores. It's the inside story of the current Godfather of New York organized crime, the one and only Don Guido Perillo. There's a murder suspect for you!"

"I couldn't tell you how often I've heard the words, 'I had no idea that he was thinking of taking his own life.' "

"If it were suicide, where's the weapon he used? I saw no gun. There's no rope. No knife."

"He might have taken poison."

"Trust me! Jonathan did not travel all the way up from the city to kill himself in my boathouse. He hated the countryside. He said if he wanted to admire a tree or a boulder, he could find all he needed in Central Park."

"You had no idea Mr. Dodge was on your property?"

"You could've knocked me over with the proverbial feather. I understood he was out of the country. I can't imagine why he'd cancel that trip and tear himself away from his book to come up here. We're alike on that score. Once a book grabs me, I hate to be dragged from it. This may sound callous, Miss Flynn, but I don't know what's upset me more this morning. Jonathan dead in my boathouse or being interrupted in my work."

Walking ahead of her, Griffith appeared exactly as she imagined an author. Sand-colored hair long overdue at a barber's came down in back to the frayed collar of a faded blue denim shirt. Pants were brown corduroy. The sweater's sleeves were ragged at the elbows. She placed his age at fifty-something. He walked briskly.

"Tell me how you think Dodge's body wound up in your boathouse," she said, striving to keep pace.

"Correct me if I'm wrong, but isn't it the first rule of homicide investigation that the one who reports the murder is likely to be the one who 'done' it? Since I did not kill Jonathan, it must follow that someone hoped to pin his murder on me."

"Who would want to do that? And why?"

"When you catch him, ask him and let me know. Okay?"

"How long did you know Dodge?"

When a pause for a second attempt to light a match failed before the wind, Griffith stared down forlornly at the pipe, tamped it with a fingertip already dirty with ash from previous tampings, and grumbled, "Can you carry on this interrogation in the house?"

"This is not an interrogation, Mr. Griffith."

He walked again, but slower. "How long did I know Jonathan? More than thirty years. He'd come down to New York City from a newspaper in Boston where he'd just covered the Boston Strangler murders. He was peddling a book on the case to publishers. He got a contract and a modest advance. I'd just gotten out of the Army and had come to the city to look up a buddy who had promised me a job writing news at a television network. A few weeks after I was hired, Jonathan came on board to earn a living until his book was published. Over the years we played journalistic tag all over the globe. We were in Vietnam together, Moscow, Washington, all over the Middle East, Pakistan, the Afghan war. While we covered the Cold War hot spots, taking turns at scooping one another, we were writing books on the side. He cranked out nonfiction. I dabbled in spies, then detectives. We quit chasing news a few years ago."

"Why was that?"

"I was just sick and tired of it. The nature of the news business had changed. 'Who, what, where, when, why, and how?' had been subordinated to 'What's it cost?' I felt a growing disgust and dejection over my journalistic reputation being put in the hands of accountants. And I looked around me at the new faces and found myself surrounded by kids who couldn't spell or write a decent sentence, who think rock 'n' roll is really music, and who believe history began with their birthday. As for Jonathan, he finally wrote a book that sold. It was a memoir of Vietnam. But not the war. It was about an intrepid Saigon police detective who was investigating a homicide. In the midst of wholesale killing on the battlefield, this cop was busting his ass to track down the murderer of some government flunky. Can you believe it?"

"Being a cop myself, certainly. Did he arrest him?"

"Hell, no. But that didn't bother Jonathan. His book sold half a million in hardcover. My novel that same year was a stab at a spy story. It sold a tenth of that. In *paperback.*"

"If it will make you feel better, I bought one of 'em."

Griffith spun around with a grin. "Did you really?"

"It was called *Echoes from the Woods*. You wrote in the preface that you took the title from a Russian proverb."

" 'As one shouts into a wood, so the echo replies.' That's what the Cold War was all about. Shouting in the woods."

"I liked it very much, despite your hero's cynicism."

"You can't have been a journalist and not turn into a cynic. Is it the same for a police detective?"

"Ask me a few years from now."

"I can't tell you how thrilled I am to meet someone who not only bought my first book but *read* it. You'd be surprised how many people who know authors personally don't actually read their books. Of course, they don't buy them, either. They expect to get free copies. People think authors get as many of their books as they want for free. Well, an author's lucky if he gets a dozen. After that, he buys 'em."

"Perhaps one day you can autograph *Echoes from the Woods* for me," Flynn said as they entered the house.

"Excuse the mess," he said. "I'm still unpacking. This is to be my office and library."

Scattered with cardboard cartons, the wood-paneled room was barely furnished. An interesting cane swivel chair stood before a desk that held a computer whose cursor seemed to be winking at her from a screen that cast a greenish light. A brown leather Chesterfield couch and a green wingback chair flanked a large Oriental carpet intricately woven with a golden dragon against a red and blue background. The huge stone hearth had a good fire going. Rubbing her hands, she exclaimed, "I adore an open fire. It may be spring, but you'd never know it this morning."

"It was the hearth more than anything else that made up my mind to buy this dump," Griffith said, stirring the fire with a poker. "There's something elemental about a stack of wood aburning. A blaze such as this calls up vestiges of the primeval in us. The ocean, a starry night, the screech of an unseen bird in the woods are echoes of the time when our species first walked the earth."

She turned, smiling. "The good old days when any man who wanted a woman bashed her on the head with a club and dragged her back to his cave by the hair?"

He laughed and sat on the couch, stretching long legs toward the fire, while she took the wingback and let her eyes roam over the array of a life's possessions in the midst of being moved from one abode to another. Most of the boxes, she assumed, held books. The sides of two had "FRAGILE" on them in the bold red ink of a wide-tipped Magic Marker, and "KITCHEN/DINING ROOM" in black. In a corner stood a massive console radio in the elegantly streamlined Art Deco style of the 1930s.

Crossing the room to examine it, she asked, "Does it work?"

"If you plug it in and turn it on."

Twisting an ornate brass dial, she made a long brass arrow sweep in an arc across a plate engraved with numbers. "Would I hear an old-time program? A soap opera, perhaps? Jack Benny?"

"I happen to be a mystery writer, Miss Flynn. You'd more than likely catch 'The Shadow' or 'Gangbusters.' In your case, you'd probably prefer 'Mr. District Attorney,' which was one of my favor-

16

ites when I was a kid. I can still recite the opening."

Stroking the sleek dark wood of the cabinet, she said, "I'd love to hear it."

" 'And it shall be my duty as District Attorney,' " Griffith recited in a forced stentorian voice, " 'not only to prosecute to the limit of the law all persons accused of crimes perpetrated within this county, but to defend with equal vigor the rights and privileges of all its citizens.' " He barked a laugh. "I had not a clue as to what most of those words meant. But I sure loved that show. The investigator for the D.A. on the program was also Irish. Name of Harrington. Now here I am talking to a real-life D.A.'s investigator. Life imitates art. Small world, huh?"

"Smaller than you suppose. In college, my senior thesis was on the subject of crime programs on radio and television. Though I was not around to hear your favorite show on the air, I did listen to a few recordings of it. It *was* a good program. I also liked the fact that the woman on the show—"

"Miss Miller, played by Vicki Vola! Isn't that a great name?"

"I liked that Miss Miller wasn't just a secretary. She got involved in each case. Very advanced thinking for the 1940s."

"Did the show give you the idea to become an investigator for a district attorney?"

"That's another story. A long one."

"After you've solved Jonathan's murder, I'd like to hear it. I don't know which has been a greater shock to me, Miss Flynn; finding Jonathan dead, or finding him dead up here in the middle of the sticks."

"When I was growing up, my friends and I used to play on this property," she said. "But we stayed clear of the house."

"Were you afraid Ilona Troy would come out and grab you, like the witch in a fairy tale?"

"The old girl was dead by then. And the estate was going to seed. We were scared the house was haunted."

Griffith's chuckle sent a gust of smoke billowing toward her. "Marvelous! Is it?"

"Local lore held that Benedict Arnold had been seen wandering around looking for General Washington," she went on. "Others claimed to have glimpsed Major André's corpse hanging by the neck from a rope thrown over a porch rafter."

"I assure you, I have encountered only the living around the place. Until this morning in the boathouse."

"Even without ghosts, I still find this house fascinating. Would you show me the rest of it?"

"Do you think you might find more bodies? Further victims of my homicidal impulses?"

"Let's just say that I would like to satisfy my unrequited childhood curiosity."

He shot to his feet. "I'll be delighted to give you a tour. But there's not much to see. It's got four bedrooms but only one bathroom upstairs in the back facing the river, and downstairs this room, a very ancient kitchen, a dining room, and a parlor. All are desperately in need of renovation. There's one damp and musty cellar with a dirt floor that I'm going to have to cement over and an attic with a leaky roof. Both are going to cost me an arm and a leg to fix."

Leaving the library, they passed through a shabby but still grand foyer at the front of the house and entered the parlor. It and the adjoining dining room were bare of furnishings.

"I'm trying to decide whether to buy all new things or go the antique route," he said. "But if the place really is haunted, I suppose I'd be wise to buy cheap. I wouldn't want a frolicsome spirit turning over my expensive chairs and tables or smashing a priceless souvenir of my fascinating life. I save everything and then I plaster the walls with them. My friends say my apartment in the city is like a museum. But I do not believe in sticking memories in drawers and closets."

"Isn't that a problem for Mrs. Griffith? All that dusting."

"There is no Mrs. Griffith."

"Has there never been?"

"Like Dr. John H. Watson, I waltzed down the matrimonial aisle once. Unlike him, I chose not to repeat the experience. I used to say there are four things that will ruin one's life: A spouse, a house, a car, a pet. Well, I've got only two of them now. The car out front and this house."

"So you'll have this place all to yourself."

"Except for the ghosts."

"Surely you must have heard the ghost stories when you were considering buying the property?"

"Had I done so, I might have closed the deal sooner," Griffith said, as they ascended a gracefully curving staircase to the second floor. "That would make a terrific blurb on a book jacket: 'The author resides in a haunted house.' As to having the place to myself, the moment everyone I know heard I was setting up shop in the country, they started inviting themselves for weekends and summers. The ghosts will find the old homestead rather crowded."

She smiled. "Have you never believed in ghosts?"

"Only to the extent that they provide lucrative pickings as settings for novels of the sort cranked out by Stephen King. As for me and my books, I take my cue from Sherlock Holmes. When he set out to investigate the case of the Sussex Vampire, he said to Watson, 'This agency stands flat-footed upon the ground and there it must remain. The world is big enough for us. No ghosts need apply.' He didn't buy spectral hounds, either, as you probably recall from reading *The Hound of the Baskervilles* as a child."

"The only detectives I read about in books were Nancy Drew and Miss Jane Marple." Flynn peered into an empty, dusty bedroom. "I thought Holmes was for boys. When I did get around to him, I found myself turned off by his attitude toward my sex."

" 'Women are never to be entirely trusted—not the best of them.' "

She scowled. "Pre-*cisely!*"

"Will it assuage your feelings if I tell you he admitted to being outsmarted four times by women? He kept a photograph of the best of them."

"Miss Irene Adler. The adventuress from New Jersey."

"You have caught up on your Sherlock, I see."

Going down a long hallway affording views of more vacant rooms, she said, "Empty houses are so sad."

"And they can be dangerous. Holmes nearly got shot in the head in one. Of course, he deduced the peril and thwarted it."

"How do you feel about the theory that Holmes's attitude toward women stemmed from homosexuality?"

"Outraged. But not, as you might suppose, because I disdain homosexuals. Jonathan Dodge's being gay never bothered me."

Her eyes narrowed. "Dodge was a homosexual?"

"It was years before I found out. As to Holmes being gay, I object to the theory because it has no basis. As everyone who's read the adventures knows, he was uninterested in love and sex. He believed romantic emotion was incompatible with logic."

As Flynn looked into the last of the unfurnished rooms, Griffith lit the pipe again. "I like your tobacco," she said.

"That's rare. Most women hate the aroma of Balkan Sobranie," he said, standing aside to let her go downstairs ahead of him.

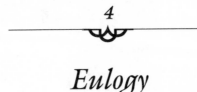

4

Eulogy

"IF YOU ASSUME that this is a homicide case," she said as they returned to the library, "can you think who might have done it? Did Dodge have enemies?"

Griffith paced the carpet, smoking avidly, then blurted, "I'm not interested in delivering Jonathan's eulogy by casting aspersions or fueling suspicions. That's your job."

She leaned against the unadorned mantel of the fireplace and smiled slyly. "I take that to mean that he did."

He threw up his arms. "What writer doesn't make enemies?"

"I'm not speaking in the generic."

Griffith alternately puffed and spoke. "Jonathan could be a horrible person. Deliberately cruel. Sadistic. He treated people poorly as a newsman, as an author, and as a friend. I assume he was the same way with his lovers. There may be a big turnout for his funeral, but there won't be very many mourners. And some of the ones who will come will do so just to make sure he is, as the Munchkins put it in *The Wizard of Oz,* 'most *sincerely* dead.' "

"Yet you and he were almost lifelong friends."

"Jonathan was a great newsman. And a better writer than I'll ever be. He was a magnificent war correspondent and an expert foreign affairs journalist, but in his heart he was still working the police beat. His book on the Boston Strangler pioneered the True Crime genre. He did books on Son of Sam, Ted Bundy, Jeffrey Dahmer, and half a dozen others."

"Did he have family?"

"Only if you count the latest in a string of live-in lovers. Jimmy something."

"Where did Dodge reside in the city?"

"He has a Gramercy Park town house and a getaway place on Fire Island. That's what half a million hardcover sales gets you. I've got a one-bedroom on the Upper West Side."

"And now your getaway spot in the country."

"Haunted and mortgaged."

"When and where did you last see Mr. Dodge?"

"Friday night at the Edgar Allan Poe Awards dinner of the Mystery Writers of America. Jonathan got the Grand Master Prize."

"Was it black tie?"

"Jonathan always took to heart the little joke printed at the bottom of the invitations: 'Dress to kill.' He thought he looked great in black. He does, too. Even dead in my boathouse."

"You said your friends knew that you'd bought this place. Had any of them been here?"

"A man named Wiggins has been here on a couple of occasions, keeping me from making mistakes in the buying. He's well informed in real estate matters. He owns a bookstore in the city. Mystery books, of course. As to others who knew that I'd acquired this property, it's possible one or two or maybe all of them could have decided to have a looksee on their own. They're all pretty nosey. We mystery writers are. At heart, we're all frustrated detectives. Being historic, the place is marked on tourist maps."

"If it turns out Dodge was murdered the night of your awards dinner, given the fact that he's wearing a tuxedo," Flynn said as she returned to the wingback chair, "might someone at the dinner have had a motive for murder?"

"The grand ballroom of the Sheraton Center Hotel was brimming with people who make their living coming up with motives for homicide. Well, *some* of them make a living doing it. But the way Jonathan was behaving that night, murdering him probably crossed everyone's mind. With two exceptions."

She looked up, interested. "Oh? Who and why?"

"They were guests of this year's dinner chairman, the same Wiggins I told you about. They had just been introduced to Jonathan and therefore had not known him long and well enough to want to see him dead. But those two were not the murdering type."

"You can look at someone and spot who is not the murdering type?"

"In this case, yes. They were the Chief of Detectives of the New York Police Department and his aide de camp."

PART TWO

A Dark and Stormy Night

Where is the ingenuity in unravelling a web which you yourself have woven for the express purpose of unravelling?

—EDGAR ALLAN POE

5

A Knotty Problem

ON FRIDAY NIGHT the Usual Suspects bookstore had offered to Detective Sergeant John Bogdanovic a warm, cozy, and comfortable obscurity, a kind of drowsy dusk stabbed by cones of light from green-shaded library lamps placed here and there while a pungent, pervasive drift of tobacco smoke eddied and fumed like fog. Based on Christopher Morley's "Parnassus at Home," the Usual Suspects differed from that store in the nature of the books. Parnassus had been stuffed with the ghosts of all great literature. The Usual Suspects limited itself to the purveying of murderers, thieves, thugs, kidnappers, blackmailers, poisoners, muggers, cutpurses, and an ever-expanding modern retinue of sinister creatures, malign presences, and villains who constituted that highest of intoxicants, the mystery story.

"This is what I wish created," Wiggins had declared to his architect and interior designer. Flipping open a well-thumbed copy of Morley's *The Haunted Bookshop,* he had stabbed a pudgy forefinger upon a description of how two stories of an old house had been made into one, with the lower space divided into alcoves. Above, a gallery ran around the wall and carried books up to the ceiling. "The only change from the plan that I require," he added, "is a wonderful spiral staircase."

Choice of location for the bookstore had been dictated by the history of the house. As buildings went in New York—and they went at an alarming rate, to be replaced by appallingly inferior edifices—the house at Beekman Place boasted a colorful past. In its earliest days it had become notorious as the locale of the ax murder of Cleopatra Ducoyne by Stanley Gordon, a remarkably adept deceiver of vulnerable, wealthy women. In the Prohibition era, it had been a speakeasy belonging to mobster Owney Madden. The late 1930s saw it used as a rendezvous for a cell of literary Communists and fellow travelers, including, allegedly, Dashiell Hammett. During World War II, it served GIs as a whorehouse. The fifties brought apartmental subdividing and no known crimes. But in the sixties the basement had housed a Weatherman bomb factory.

"How could such an illustrious address be anything but the digs of a mystery bookstore?" Wiggins asked when the property came onto the market in the early 1970s. After tearing out the subdivisions, he had shared the floors above the store with a procession of alluring but temporary young men and permanently with a hound named Toby and a black cat called Moriarty.

Certainly, no human being could have been better suited to the role of owner of the Usual Suspects than Wiggins, nor looked the part. Going about wintry city streets enveloped in a tweedy Inverness cloak, its cape billowing, and topped by a deerstalker, he could not venture very far from the establishment without being greeted with various versions of "How are you today, Mr. Holmes?" despite the fact that Holmes was tall and slender, with a hawkish countenance. Pumpkin-faced Wiggins weighed over three hundred pounds. When not out of doors, which was most of the time, he could be found lounging in a commodious blue armchair in his office, his huge body wrapped in a scarlet Oriental robe with golden dragons, and his amazingly demure feet tucked into ornate Persian slippers. The only occasions on which he did not leave the store reluctantly were the Baker Street Irregulars dinner in January and the Edgar Allan Poe Awards in May.

A STUDY IN PATIENCE, Sergeant Bogdanovic of the New York City Police Department observed Wiggins from an enormous antique chair with rich blue brocade upholstery and mahogany arms ending in the carved heads of hounds baring fangs. The bookstore owner was having trouble with his black bow tie. Looking around the office at the rear of the bookstore, Bogdanovic found himself faced on all sides by images of Sherlock Holmes. Obscuring the walls and cluttering tables and shelves were hundreds of old movie posters and lobby cards, photographs of actors who had portrayed Holmes on film, television, and stage, busts, statuettes, walking sticks, plates, saucers, teacups and teapots, beer steins, coffee mugs, tobacco humidors, key rings, letter openers, ashtrays, cigarette lighters, and other icons to the Sleuth of Baker Street.

Only the uppermost shelf of the rolltop desk from which Wiggins ran his bookish emporium had been exempted from homage. Upon it stood a small, glowering portrait in porcelain of Edgar Allan Poe, the central figure of the evening's festivities.

"My boss is thrilled about being invited to your dinner," said the detective. "I imagine he's had his tuxedo on since this afternoon. More than likely, he's already waiting for us in front of his apartment house."

Wiggins attempted another knot. "It's the least I could have done to repay Chief Goldstein and you for the help you provided to me in resolving the ballistics problem in my modest little mystery novel. I was afraid that no one would accept that one bullet could do what it had to do if the plot were to work. I dreaded scoffing comparisons to the single-bullet explanation in the assassination of President Kennedy. But I have a precedent in Sherlock Holmes. Dr. Watson was struck by just such a bullet. It seems to have wounded both his shoulder and leg."

"Bullets can take very strange turns."

Wiggins dropped his arms to his sides and turned envious and exasperated eyes toward the rebuke of Bogdanovic's perfect bow tie. "You seem to understand these damn things, Sergeant. Help!"

Reaching around Wiggins's enormous neck, Bogdanovic's nimble fingers deftly executed a perfect bow.

"I wonder, Sergeant," Wiggins said as he donned an enormous jacket, "if one might find in police department records any case in which someone was murdered by being strangled with a bow tie? Or a cummerbund?" He quaked with laughter. "I believe I've hit on an idea for a novel. It could be entitled *The Case of the Overdressed Corpse*. I must remember to make a note about it."

"That's really amazing," Bogdanovic said, as they made their way between parallel rows of bookcases toward the front of the store. "I've always wondered where writers get their ideas. It takes a special gift to see the makings of a murder mystery in a simple thing like a bow tie."

"There is *nothing* simple about a bow tie. As for the creative process, I'm one of those persons who believes there's nothing new under the sun. It's all been done before, either by Poe or Arthur Conan Doyle. Everyone else is a copycat. Why, even the sainted Agatha Christie owned up to patterning her most famous detective, Hercule Poirot, on Sherlock Holmes. And Conan Doyle took his cues from Poe. Reading the detective story may be the normal recreation of noble minds, but the writing of them has been one long process of imitation. There are even rules for it."

"Mystery writers follow rules?"

"As diligently as you real-life detectives adhere to your police department rulebook. The creator of Philo Vance, the late S. S. Van Dine, listed twenty such rules. In no particular order, they include: no love interest; the reader must be given the same chance to figure out the solution as the detective in the story; the detective is *never* the one who done it; there can be only one character who actually solves the crime, although he or she might have a helper or helpers. And revelations on the last page for which the reader has not been prepared are *verboten*. Monsignor Ronald A. Knox, another practitioner of mystery fiction, insisted that the murderer must be mentioned in an early part of the story. But the main rule on which all crime writers agree is that all of the clues must be plainly stated and described."

"If it were only so easy in real life," the detective said, as a husky young man appeared from a storeroom carrying a stack of books.

"This is my assistant, name of William," said Wiggins. "He is in charge of my little establishment for the evening, meaning I shall probably find the cash drawer short in the morning."

"Have a pleasant time at your dinner," the boy replied.

"You just be sure to have everything ready for my reception afterward."

"You know I've had the cigars and brandy all set since this afternoon," William said, sounding a little hurt.

"The absolutely inflexible rule about writing mysteries," Wiggins continued as they left the store under threatening stormclouds, "is that the criminal must *never* get away with it. The detective story is a morality lesson. The bad guy has to be punished, if not by the law, then in some justifying manner. In the mystery genre, there is no such thing as a perfect crime."

"There aren't any in real life, either," Bogdanovic replied as he unlocked the doors of his unmarked sedan.

"Do you know, Sergeant, this is my first ride in a police car? Any chance of your turning on the siren?"

"Sorry to disappoint you. It would be against the rules."

6

The Noble Mind

AS ALL MEN DO when formally attired, the chief of detectives presented a handsome figure as he settled into the back of the car. "Drive on, Johnny," he ordered. "The game is afoot!"

Wiggins smiled knowingly. "Name the adventure in which that quote is found."

Goldstein sighed. "Elementary, my dear Wiggins! *The Abbey Grange.*"

"Tell me the adventure in which Sherlock Holmes said, 'My ultimate object is only the truth.' "

"Trick question! That was Dupin in *The Murders in the Rue Morgue,* by the author your organization does the honor of recognizing tonight."

"It's you who honor Edgar Allan Poe, Chief, and us by your presence. We merely take on fictional webs which we ourselves weave for the express purpose of daring our readers to compete with us in unraveling them. You solve real crimes and have been doing so for decades."

"The word around headquarters," Bogdanovic interjected, "is that the Chief was lead investigator in the Cain and Abel case, and that he was furious with God Almighty for letting Cain get off with probation."

Standing five feet six inches, Harvey Goldstein had barely met minimum height for a New York policeman. In the twenty-five years since donning the blue tunic of the NYPD he had lost much of his lank brown hair, acquired a pot belly, and turned to half-moon glasses for reading. After hanging the blues in a closet for good, he had risen to the top of the detective ranks and become accustomed to finding "legendary" before his name in newspaper accounts of his homicide investigations.

Yet Bogdanovic had discovered that although the most famous detective in the history of the force was dauntingly informed on a vast array of the most arcane and technical subjects related to crime, his general knowledge and interest in subjects other than criminology proved to be minimal. When not reading the official reports flowing across his desk, he was likely to be found in a commodious yellow chair in the living room of his apartment, lost in a mystery novel.

"Do you read murder mysteries, Sergeant?" he had asked while interviewing Bogdanovic for a position carried on the police department personnel chart as Personal Assistant to the Chief of Detectives. "If not, you are making a bad mistake. You cannot learn the art of murder from a textbook. In calling murder an art, I do not refer to the run-of-the-mill saloon killings, nor Old Lady Smith using her butcher knife to settle things with Old Man Smith. I speak of those rare situations in which murder isn't so obvious as to practically solve itself. No. I speak of clever, cunning, premeditated murder, which can be brought to book only through *detection*. From this day on, Sergeant, in addition to your responsibilities as my driver and overall factotum, I expect you to hone your detectional skills by studying crime fiction. After work this evening I shall introduce you to just the man to get you started. He owns a bookstore. His name is Wiggins."

Five years later, as a clot of crosstown traffic compelled Bogdanovic to make a sudden stop, Wiggins grumbled, "This city is getting more impossible every day. At moments like this I find it easy to hate the modern age. Take me back to that simpler era when, as Vincent Starrett described it, 'Outside, the hansoms rattle through the rain, and Moriarty plans his latest devilry. Within, the sea coal flames upon the hearth and Holmes and Watson take their well-won ease. So they will live for all that love them well: in a romantic chamber of the heart, in a nostalgic country of the mind, where it is always 1895.' "

"That is a charming thought," Bogdanovic said. "But weren't the streets full of horseshit?"

Goldstein groaned. "Despite all our efforts to civilize the man,

Johnny Bogdanovic still hasn't got a romantic bone in him. He's one of the computer generation. He doesn't have a brain; his skull is equipped with an expanded-megabyte hard drive. The games he plays are strictly the video variety. I'm afraid he'll never appreciate ours. You may argue till you're blue in the face, but he will never accept what you and I regard as canonical truths, Wiggins, that Sherlock Holmes was the world's first private consulting detective, Dr. John H. Watson was his chronicler, and Arthur Conan Doyle was Watson's literary agent. Any attempt to persuade the man at the steering wheel of this car that the literary invention of Edgar Allan Poe is the normal recreation of the noble mind is an exercise in futility."

Wiggins fished a cherrywood pipe with a long, gently curved stem from his pocket. "I trust, Sergeant, that there is enough of the romantic in you that I may say of you by evening's end, as Holmes said to Watson in *The Mazarin Stone,* 'You have not, I hope, learned to despise my pipe and my lamentable tobacco?' "

"No need to worry about me griping about smoking. One of the requirements of keeping my job is making sure the boss has got a supply of tobacco on hand. The anti-smoking movement has its work cut out if they try to take away his pipe."

"If anyone dared to demand that I prohibit smoking in my store," said Wiggins as the car turned left from Fifty-third Street onto Seventh Avenue, "I'd ask, 'With whom would you prefer to spend an evening? The Surgeon General or Sherlock Holmes?' "

Invoking a privilege afforded by a blue police department identification card in the front window, Bogdanovic parked in a prohibited zone in front of the Sheraton Central Hotel.

"I'm no author," Goldstein said, stepping from the car into a throng of elegantly clad men and women flowing toward the hotel, oblivious to flashes of lightning. "But it seems to me that this evening would make a nice setting for a whodunit. All these experts in the art of murder. One of them winds up dead."

Wiggins curled a weighty arm about Goldstein's shoulder and laughed. "Chief, you are going to fit right in."

7

Suspicious Characters

FOLLOWING WIGGINS AND GOLDSTEIN across the hotel lobby to the escalators, Bogdanovic merged with a crowd of tuxedoed men and elegantly gowned women.

"Have you ever seen so many suspicious characters in one place in all your life, gentlemen?" Wiggins asked.

"We *are* policemen," Bogdanovic retorted. "We lock up shady people all the time."

"Excluding jails. The incarcerated do not count. I meant, walking around free. I dare say there has never been such a concentration of sheer criminal intellect since Professor James Moriarty paid an unexpected visit to the consulting room at 221B Baker Street."

Goldstein chuckled. " 'All that I have to say to you has already crossed your mind.' "

"We have been gathering like this to celebrate ourselves and our peculiar fascination since 1945," Wiggins continued as they ascended to another lobby on the second floor. "The only organization which has been around longer than Mystery Writers of America is the Baker Street Irregulars, formed in 1934. That is, in this country. The granddaddy of them all is London's Detection Club. It was founded by G. K. Chesterton in 1928. Nowadays you can find such groups almost anywhere, dedicated to the exaltation of one fictional sleuth or another. If you dote on Nero Wolfe, for example, there's a band of aficiandos here in this fair city called, naturally, the Wolfe Pack. The Mystery Writers of America differs from those groups in a singular aspect. All the people you'll be meeting this evening love mystery, of course, but they are even more dedicated to the proposition that crime does not pay . . .

enough. The bar is through the door on our right, fellas. As soon as we are sufficiently armed, I'll introduce you around."

Presently, clutching a Brandy Alexander and pressed by the boisterous throng at the bar, Wiggins swayed against Bogdanovic. Feeling the bulge of what could only be a shoulder holster under the sergeant's jacket, he whispered, "You are amongst friends, Sergeant. Why the artillery?"

Bogdanovic squeezed his arm against his side. "Like they say in those credit card commercials, I never leave home without it."

"Is that a departmental regulation?"

"No. It's personal. When I signed on as aide to the Chief of Detectives, I made up my mind that in this era when any public figure might become a tempting target for anyone for any reason in any place, whenever Goldstein ventured out and about in public I would not consume alcohol, leave his side, or be found without my weapon."

Wiggins's eyes glinted merrily. "What do you pack?"

"It's a Glock nine-millimeter, fifteen-shot automatic."

"Heavy artillery," Wiggins said with a glance at Goldstein as he waited patiently for a waiter to pour a scotch and water. "I'm sure he must be grateful for such dedication."

Bogdanovic shrugged. "In his own way."

After a sip of the brandy, Wiggins said, "I sense an amusing anecdote."

Bogdanovic glanced at Goldstein. "On the first day I drove him to an appointment, we came to a red light. Well, I wanted to hit the lights and siren and go right on through. He would not have it. While we waited for the signal to change, he leaned over the front seat and said, 'Sergeant, suppose a gang of terrorists surrounded us at this instant, determined to take the Chief of Detectives hostage. What could you possibly do about it?' "

Wiggins grinned in anticipation. "This is so deliciously vicious. What was your answer?"

"I turned around," Bogdanovic continued, with a slight smile that dimpled his cheeks, "I looked at him straight in the eyes and said, 'That's easy, sir. I would make damn certain they didn't take you alive.' "

As rumbling laughter shook Wiggins's houndish jowls and

made Jell-O of his enormous stomach, Goldstein eased away from the crowded bar and rejoined them. "What's the joke, boys? Not about me, I trust?"

Before Bogdanovic could reply, a mellifluously baritone voice boomed behind him. "Wiggins! How's trade in fake first editions?"

Turning, Bogdanovic found himself face to face with a man whose bulky physique and wide shoulders were magnified by the sweep of a blue opera cape. He grasped a walking stick capped by what appeared to be a miniature of the Maltese Falcon in silver. Brown hair suggested rusting steel wool. A broad furrowed face seemed hewn for the purpose of accenting deeply set blue eyes. Twinkling without warmth, they peered probingly at Goldstein, then lit in recognition. "I know you," he exclaimed. "You're Chief of Detectives Goldstein, and the guy with the iron tucked into his armpit is the intrepid young sleuth who has been your trusty right hand in several of your recent more celebrated cases, Sergeant somebody or other."

"John Bogdanovic," Bogdanovic said curtly.

"This rude character is Jonathan Dodge," Wiggins announced, pointing with his brandy glass. "Tonight he is to be crowned this year's Grand Master. If you have read any of his books, you will have recognized that he is already a legend in his own mind."

"A word of advice, gentlemen, concerning those whom you will be meeting this evening," replied Dodge. "People are not always what they say they are."

Goldstein shrugged. "Thank you very much, Mr. Dodge. But I've been a cop since I was twenty-two years old, so your advice, well intended as it may be, is hardly news."

"Consider Wiggins," Dodge continued. "As I presume you know, 'Wiggins' was the name of the leader of the little band of street arabs Holmes employed as an unofficial police force, the original Baker Street Irregulars, first introduced in *The Sign of Four*. The rotund figure before us not only claims Wiggins to be his *real* name, he purports to be a descendant of an actual youth who provided the inspiration for the character in the canon."

"*Purports?*" Wiggins thundered. "Are you calling me a liar?"

"I'm simply asserting a Sherlockian truth. 'It is always awkward doing business with an alias.'"

Another voice intruded. "If this is a quiz, Jonathan," it said sharply, "you are insulting the intelligence of these men. *The Blue Carbuncle*. The *Strand* magazine. January 1892. Jonathan, it's *elementary*."

Wiggins's great head turned slowly to find a tall, sandy-haired figure holding a champagne glass. "Chief Goldstein, Sergeant Bogdanovic," Wiggins said, "permit me to introduce Morgan Griffith, another scribbler in the vineyards of murder, mayhem, and mystery."

Jonathan Dodge also turned. "Hello, Griffith," he said. "I see you still possess the knack for butting in."

Griffith raised his glass as if to offer a toast. "Good to see you, too, Jonathan. How's tricks? Or are you unaccompanied? Have you decided to go straight, at last?"

"Believe it or not, these two are very old friends," Wiggins interjected. "Pay no attention to their jibes."

"*The* Morgan Griffith?" asked Goldstein.

"The one and only," answered Dodge.

"I've read all your books, Mr. Griffith," Goldstein said. "I hope you've got a new one in the pipeline."

"I've been kicking one around for months. I don't have the knack for grinding out one a year like Jonathan Dodge. He's a wellspring of inspiration to the rest of us. If it's autumn, you can be sure there'll be a new Jonathan Dodge blockbuster on the way, just in time for Christmas giving, of course."

"What about that, Mr. Dodge? Are you at work? Are you at liberty to tell us what your next book will be?" Goldstein asked.

"I'm returning to the scene of the crime, so to speak."

"Jonathan, how cryptic," said Wiggins.

"I'm leaving the country tomorrow for further research. The odyssey will also carry me to London, where I intend to call at the Public Records Office to resolve the Wiggins question."

"Be my guest," huffed Wiggins across an uplifted but nearly drained glass of Brandy Alexander.

"If all goes well," Dodge said, as his eyes shifted between the four men and settled on Griffith, "I expect to come back to New York with the answer to an intriguing question of identity that I'm sure will be of interest to everyone at this dinner."

"What does it matter what Wiggins calls himself?" Griffith demanded. "In this country a man can go by any name he chooses. Isn't that correct, Chief?"

"As long as it's not an alias taken for an illicit purpose."

"If the purpose isn't illicit," Dodge said with a wink, "why go to all the trouble?" The searching eyes turned to the crowd at the bar. "Now, if you'll excuse me, gentlemen, I'm lagging way behind the mob. I went along with my doctor and gave up smoking, but I told him if I had to give up drinking I'd rather be dead. He said I would be. A dead drunk."

As he drifted to the bar, Bogdanovic asked, "What's with the cane and the cape?"

Wiggins sniffed. "Affectations. And he believes that if he were to check them, they'd be stolen. I can see purloining the stick. It's silver. The cape is cheap. Now, may I propose that we all adjourn to the dining room and search out our table? They'll be calling all the hogs to the trough soon. Avoid the rush!"

8

Our Lady of the Mysteries

"HOTEL BALLROOMS we have known, eh, Chief?" Wiggins commented as they entered the dining room. "Table Two is us. We shall have ringside seats for the presentations of the Edgars. Unfortunately, we'll also be too conspicuous to sneak out when the speeches ramble on too long, as they usually do. With the rare exception, no writer should be allowed to speak in public. I'm one of the exceptions, naturally."

Bogdanovic paged through a program and wondered why no such recognition existed for cops. Why was there not a festive banquet to honor the best detective in a homicide case, the best cop on a beat, the best parking-ticket writer?

Presently, as Wiggins introduced those who would share Table Two, Bogdanovic recognized names he had read in the program, either as authors of articles or listed in the awards categories. Taking the chair to his left, Margaret Tinney had been nominated for best fact crime for her account of the crimes of a cannibalistic serial killer, entitled *Six and Twenty Corpses Baked in a Pie*. Looking as dowdy and innocent as his maiden aunt Helen, she immediately turned to him. "What wonderful luck to have a policeman here," she exclaimed. "You can help me with a problem I've run into in the novel I'm working on."

"I'd be happy to," he said. "If I can."

"Where's the best spot on the East Side of town to dump a body so that it will not be discovered for at least twenty-four hours?"

"That's easy. Just prop your corpse against any building. Everyone will assume it's a homeless person and walk right by."

She clutched his arm tightly. "Oh, Sergeant, that is such a cruel thing to think about your fellow New Yorkers. But, my, yes. That is *very good.*"

"Be sure to send her a bill, Sergeant," said a deeply tanned man with a mane of white hair seated on his right. He had been introduced as Alexander Somerfield. Listed in the program as the author of a string of Cold War espionage novels, he was nominated for an Edgar for a novel entitled *I Spy You.* "If Maggie thinks you will work for free, she'll be on your case for further advice all the time. And you won't get so much as an autographed copy of the book you'll have ended up writing for her. My advice to you, sir, is save your very original ideas for your own book."

"But it's not original," Bogdanovic replied earnestly. "It really happened. Last year, the body of a seventy-year-old man was there for four days. We arrested his sixty-year-old wife for murder two days later when we located her in Miami Beach with her eighteen-year-old lover. I believe there's to be a TV movie based on the case."

"How nice. You'll be able to see yourself," said Somerfield.

"I'm afraid my work doesn't leave me much time to watch TV. I've got a real slave driver for a boss."

"And who would that be?"

"He's to your left. Chief of Detectives Harvey Goldstein."

Somerfield turned slightly, smiled, and turned back. "I take it you're a bodyguard. That explains the pistol under your coat."

Wiggins blared, "You might as well tote that Glock out in the open, Sergeant B. There are no secrets in this room."

"Are you at work on a book, Mr. Somerfield?" Goldstein said.

"I recently completed a novel."

"What's the title?"

Griffith touched Goldstein's sleeve. "Oh, Chief, you have asked the impossible. Alex never talks about his books in advance of publication. Nobody knows the title, save Alex's editor. And there she is in the doorway! Right on cue."

"What an arresting-looking woman," whispered Goldstein as he gazed at a tiny but matronly white-haired figure in a black and white gown. Poised in the arched doorway as her eyes surveyed the gala scene before them, she appeared hesitant about entering. "She looks as though she's just stepped out of an illustration by Edward Gorey."

Wiggins turned his pumpkin head slowly and peered across the room through slits of eyes almost lost in fleshy cheeks. "That formidable lady is Elvira Eveland," he answered gaily. "She's the doyenne of the whodunit. The roster of crime writers that woman has discovered in her editing career is a *Who's Who* of the genre, going all the way back to the Depression. I call her 'Our Lady of the Mysteries.' Come. You must meet her. You too, Sergeant B."

As Bogdanovic towered before her while Wiggins introduced them, sharp green eyes twinkled up at him. "My, what a long drink of water you are, Sergeant," she said as her arm entwined his. "I happen to adore tall guys. When they're also dark and handsome, so much the better. Is that a gun in your coat? I hope so. There are so many at this shindig who need a slug of lead. Or two. Or six. Be a darling and fetch me a drink. Scotch, please. Neat."

"I'll go," said Wiggins. "Sergeant B is on duty, Elvira."

"How fascinating. Is our little affair to become like Rick's place in *Casablanca?* Will there be an arrest here tonight? Am I the lucky dog?"

At that moment, Jonathan Dodge stepped to her side. "I have a bone to pick with you, Elvira. And you do know what I mean."

"Not now, Jonathan," Eveland said with a frown and a tightened hold on Bogdanovic's bicep. "This is hardly the time. Be a nice lad and come to my office Monday. We'll lunch at the Algonquin."

Dodge shook his head violently. "I'm going away tomorrow. We have to settle this business tonight. In fact, this *instant.*"

She let go of Bogdanovic's arm. "If I'm not back in five minutes call the coppers."

9

Agent von Bork

"POOR ELVIRA. To be in the clutches of that dreadful man. Of course, we are in her debt for saving us from having to deal with him for even a second."

Myron Frank smiled in a manner that always reminded Wiggins of descriptions by Dr. Watson of Scotland Yard's Inspector Lestrade: rat-faced, ferretlike, dark-eyed, little, lean, and sallow.

"Wouldn't you agree, Wiggins?" Frank continued, pointing a glass of gin and tonic at the door through which Dodge and Elvira Eveland had departed, "that Jonathan Dodge is a most remarkable character, worthy of an entry in the *Guinness Book of World Records*? The man possesses the singular quality of lighting up the room merely by leaving it. Imagine the effect if he left the world."

Amused beady eyes flicked sideways from Wiggins to the two men flanking him.

"Are you going to introduce your guests, Wiggins?" Frank asked. "Or must I consult the names on the seating lists in the program and deduce their identities? That *is* one of the games we play at this dinner, gentlemen. Who's who?"

"These gentlemen are Harvey Goldstein, Chief of Detectives, NYPD, and his assistant, Sergeant John Bogdanovic," Wiggins replied. "Fellas, this is Myron Frank, known to members of the Baker Street Irregulars as 'Agent von Bork,' his investiture."

Bogdanovic's brow wrinkled into a puzzled frown. "Excuse me. What's an investiture?"

Goldstein groaned and rolled his eyes. "Johnny, you do know what the Baker Street Irregulars is?"

"Sure. It's a Sherlock Holmes club."

"*The* club," Wiggins corrected. "Persons deemed worthy are bestowed with an honorary name taken from the Holmes stories. One also gets a shilling coin at the time. But *exceptionally worthy* individuals get two shillings."

Bogdanovic could not suppress a giggle. "How many shillings do you have?"

Wiggins beamed. "I'm proud to report I got two this year."

"Much to Jonathan Dodge's chagrin," Frank said darkly. "I'm surprised to observe he's still talking to you. I understand he is determined to prove that Wiggins is not your real name. If so, will you have to give back the shillings, I wonder?"

"Excuse me, Mr. Frank," Bogdanovic interjected impatiently. "But what is the significance in your investiture as Agent von Bork? Or isn't there one?"

"The agent von Bork was a spy. I'm a literary agent. It's a rather lame joke."

"Being a literary agent, he spends his time at these dinners calculating whether there might be a percentage for himself in meeting the new faces," Wiggins said with a cold smile. "He used to represent Jonathan Dodge. Indeed, he was his only client, that is until Jonathan gave him the old heave-ho a couple of weeks ago. The reason remains tantalizingly obscure. Would you care to write an end to the mystery for us, Myron?"

"I assure you it was an amicable parting."

"Believe that, fellas, and I've got a bridge to Brooklyn I'd like to sell you," laughed Wiggins.

"Not to mention a bunch of first editions in that backroom in your bookstore, signed by the greatest names in mystery and detection literature," snapped Frank, rattling the ice in his gin and tonic. "All of whom happen to be fortuitously deceased."

"I presume you are aware that your ex-client receives the Grand Master award this evening," Wiggins said, unfazed. "Perhaps Jonathan will take a moment during his acceptance speech to dispel the mystery of the Great Schism."

Frank drained his glass. "All this must strike you policemen as pretty childish," he said, turning aside to deposit it on the nearest table. "The gossip of bookish people like Wiggins and me has to be small potatoes to men who deal every day with the realities of a violent city. Are you engaged in an investigation at the moment? If so, I'd love to hear about it."

Wiggins lifted a pudgy left hand to his left ear. "That sound you hear," he said, "is Myron's mental calculator toting up what he can make for you off the hardcover, the paperback, worldwide rights, first- and second-subsidiary rights, books-on-audio, and, of course, movie, TV and home video sales. After his fifteen percent off the top."

"I'm no writer, Mr. Frank," Goldstein said.

"The memoirs of Chief of Detectives Harvey Goldstein," said Bogdanovic dreamily. "That's not a bad idea, boss."

"There'd be only one thing rarer than a Goldstein first edition," the chief replied. "A Goldstein *second* edition. No, I'll leave the writing to the people who know what they're doing. And who have something to say."

Frank flattened a hand to his chest as if he were suffering a heart attack and gasped, "Good Lord! If the book world were to adopt that philosophy, we would all go out of business for a lack of authors."

Looking past Frank as Goldstein and Wiggins laughed, Bogdanovic observed Jonathan Dodge return to the room. Brushing by wordlessly, he made his way to a chair at Table One. A moment behind him came Elvira Eveland. Also without speaking but looking terribly pale, she proceeded directly to her place at Table Two and seemed oblivious to the hefty young man in a Norfolk tweed jacket, with a trim brown beard and shock of long, unruly hair, who stood to greet her.

10

Art in the Blood

"OH GOOD, I see we have been graced with the companionship of Vernon Ney, artist *extraordinaire.*"

That Wiggins should know the young man came as no surprise to Bogdanovic. By now he assumed Wiggins knew everyone.

"Vern is recipient of no less than three Edgar awards," Wiggins continued as Bogdanovic resumed his chair between Elvira Eveland and Margaret Tinney. "Two are for deliciously malevolent novels of Gothic suspense and horror set against a background of art and artists that make *The Picture of Dorian Gray* seem like a kiddy bedtime story. The other Edgar is a special citation for his body of work as designer of dust jackets. A double-barreled talent—authoring and painting. He is in the process of doing my portrait. It is to adorn the wall behind the cash register in my store. How's the work going, Vern? I do hope you're permitting the art in my soul to radiate through this singularly impressive countenance."

"As Sherlock Holmes observed," Ney replied, a smile through the neat beard giving him the look of a hirsute imp," 'Art in the blood *is* liable to take the *strangest* forms.' Emphasis mine."

"*Touché,* Wiggy," chirped Margaret Tinney.

"Go easy on the jests, you pigment-stained wretch," Wiggins replied merrily. "If the painting does not satisfy me I may take a cue from a person who shall remain nameless and not only stiff you for your fee but sue you for slander."

"Don't be coy, Wiggy. Go ahead and say the name," Elvira Eveland interjected grumpily. "It's been in *Publishers Weekly.* We all know it's Jonathan Dodge, whom I shall always remember with passion after tonight as *the* son of a bitch."

Wiggins reached out and touched her hand tenderly. "Oh my dear, what's the dirty rat done to *you?* Shall I go over there right now and punch him in the nose?"

Eveland attempted a smile. "It's nothing to concern you, my friend. I'm sure it will all be sorted out amicably."

"If it isn't and you want something done about it, let me know. I am familiar with certain circles specializing in settling matters that can't be sorted out amicably," Wiggins said. Turning to Bogdanovic, he whispered. "Sergeant B, you've probably made their acquaintance as well, at one time or another."

Leaning across the table from a chair opposite Bogdanovic, Morgan Griffith said, "No need to bring in the Mob, Wiggy. We'll just put the names of people who've got a score or two to settle with Jonathan in a hat. The one who wins the draw does the deed and the rest of us provide the lucky cuss an alibi. That'd be a case Chief Goldstein and Sergeant B could never solve."

"Don't count on it," retorted Goldstein.

Griffith reared up and back. "But how could you?" he demanded. "It's the perfect scenario for murder. The victim is someone who's hated by everyone, but your legion of suspects are all in it together, covering for one another."

"Yes, I read it already. *Murder on the Orient Express.* The funny little Belgian sleuth with an egg-shaped head solved it. I have no fear that Sergeant Johnny Bogdanovic would crack the case of the murder of Jonathan Dodge just as readily."

"Especially, my dear Griffith, since you have already told him the plot," scolded Elvira Eveland. Turning slightly to her left, she placed a tiny, cool hand on Bogdanovic's shoulder and adopted a motherly tone. "Be the darling smart young man I'm sure you are and tell us how you might go about ridding the world of a pest like Jonathan Dodge. So that you'd never be found out."

When Bogdanovic turned anxious eyes toward the chief of detectives, Goldstein chuckled. "Go ahead, Johnny. Tell them."

"It's a very simple proposition," he said calmly. "But quite cold-blooded. It would require real guts. You'd have to be wholly without a conscience."

Eveland's eyes twinkled. "Oh, I handed mine to the devil a long time ago. Before you were a glimmer in your daddy's eye."

"You don't commit one murder. You commit several. You lose the person you really want to kill in a crowd of randomly selected victims, each killed in a different manner. The homicide team would find no connection. Nothing to link the crimes. No trail to follow to the perpetrator. They would be serial killings but with no evidence to say so. The reason serial killers get caught is that they leave a psychological hallmark every time. That is the basis for all the success that's been achieved in the area of criminal profiling. If you carried out absolutely random murders using different methods, there'd be no way to draw a profile."

Eveland planted a kiss on Bogdanovic's cheek. "My dearest Sergeant, that is positively scrumptious. You and I must have a lunch one day so that I may explore that devious brain of yours at leisure. I'll pick up the check, of course."

"Lunch with you sounds terrific, Miss Eveland. . . ."

"Elvira!"

"But the New York Police Department takes a very dim view of cops who dine on the cuff. Besides, I'm an old-fashioned guy who can never feel right about a woman paying my tab."

"I'm constrained by no such inhibitions, Elvira," exclaimed Griffith. "You can take me to lunch instead. How about tomorrow? And the day after that. My lunches are wide open indefinitely."

Eveland shrugged. "You're a writer. Writers are supposed to starve."

Griffith lifted a spoon and toyed with a soggy strawberry on top of a bowl of fruit cocktail grown warm from having sat so long. "You're right as usual, Elvira. Lord knows, if I cared about food I certainly wouldn't be here."

By the time he and the others had disposed of the first course, an elegantly slender figure had wafted into the next to the last empty chair.

"Chief G, Sergeant B, this tardy creature disguising himself behind that silver-toned goatee is Oscar Pendleton," Wiggins announced. "He is the proprietor of the second most important bookstore in our fair city. He calls his little establishment on the Upper West Side 'Mysterious Doings.' He also puts out a line of books carrying the same imprint. Now that Oscar is here, we lack only Jack Bohannon. Oscar, you are *soaked.*"

Pendleton dabbed his forehead with a napkin. "There is a thunderstorm going on out there that gives a new meaning to the cliché 'dark and stormy night.' It's why I'm late. Bohannon must be caught in it, too. His car is probably stuck in a flood on the Long Island Expressway. Have I missed anything sensational?"

"Sergeant Bogdanovic discoursed on the perfect method to rid ourselves of your least favorite author," said Eveland, grinning.

Pendleton laid down the napkin. "Jonathan? Excellent."

"We band together and kill several people, each differently," Wiggins whispered. "We stick Jonathan in the middle of the crowd."

"May we count you in on the conspiracy?" asked Griffith.

"Naturally we can," Wiggins answered. "No one at this table has a more compelling motive than dear Oscar. Jonathan committed the first deadly sin. He defected to another publisher."

" 'Nothing is simpler than to kill a man,' " Pendleton said. " 'The difficulties arise in attempting to avoid the consequences.' "

"Nero Wolfe, 1938," Wiggins exclaimed. *"Too Many Cooks."*

"Exactly my point. That's the flaw in your plan. Too many cooks. The trouble with making a conspiracy is that it's only as reliable as its weakest link. As for me, I'd never enter into a plot with you, Wiggins, because you talk too much. It's part of your charm. Sooner or later you would have to blab about it."

"Is it your motion, therefore, that this ad hoc committee on the murder of Jonathan Dodge vote in favor of it being carried out solo?"

"Yes. And I move that the question be voted on immediately."

"All those in favor," said Wiggins, "signify by raising a hand."

Counting no dissenters, Bogdanovic gasped, "I can't believe what I'm seeing and hearing."

Laughter bubbled up and rippled around the table.

Slapping Bogdanovic on the back, Goldstein chuckled, "Oh, Johnny boy, they're pulling your leg!"

PART THREE

The Critic

The criminal is the creative artist; the detective only the critic.

—G. K. CHESTERTON

11

Two and Two Equal Six

SUNDAY'S CLOUDS promised to break and let the sun shine in as two men in gray jumpsuits heaved up the bulky olive green plastic body bag containing Jonathan Dodge's body from the boathouse and Morgan Griffith breathed a long, pained sigh. "It's just dawned on me," he said to Arlene Flynn, glumly. "Someone's going to have to take charge of burying him and then arrange a memorial service. I guess it'll be up to me."

The men began a careful ascent of the slippery slope.

"Do you have any idea, Miss Flynn, when I might claim the body and start making the arrangements? I assume there will have to be an autopsy."

"Yes. I can check with the coroner for you. Shall I call you at your number here at Traitor's Lair?"

"God no. I'm going back to the city right away." He fished a wallet from his pocket, removed a business card, and handed it to her. "There's no way in hell that I can get anything done, either working on the house or in my writing. I'm too shaken up. If I'm not at the New York number when you call, there'll be an answering machine."

Breathing hard, the men with the body reached the top of the hill. Below, the last of the crime scene team appeared from inside the boathouse, lugging equipment.

"This is going to sound ghoulish, Miss Flynn," Griffith said as he watched them begin their ascent, "but I've been earning my keep off the dead all my life, first as a newsman and lately by scribbling whodunits. Now all of a sudden, like the journalist in Sherlock Holmes's case of *The Six Napoleons*, I've found a murder victim dumped at my door. Poor Horace Harker was so distraught at the event that he never filed a story and got scooped by every reporter in London. As I said, this may put you off, but I'd like to get the inside story of how you go about catching whoever did it. I would like to be Dr. Watson to your Sherlock Holmes. To be in on every aspect of the investigation.

"I'd keep everything completely confidential, of course," Griffith went on. "I won't print a thing until you close the case. And I promise I won't get in your way. I might even be of some help to you. I knew Jonathan longer and better than anyone. I also know the cast of characters in his life most likely to qualify as suspects. There might even come a time that you'll be able to say to me what Holmes said to the Good Doctor. 'I'd be lost without my Boswell.' "

Frowning, Flynn tugged at her lower lip. "I'd have to clear that proposition with my boss."

"Of course! But tell him that it's been my experience that if somebody is going to be written about, it's a wise policy to see that his side of the story gets told by *him.*"

Her frown faded. "I'll pass along that advice."

He smiled. "I can't ask more than that."

Going round to the front of the house, they fell silent as the body was eased into the back of the coroner's black station wagon.

Benson's sedan and Deputy Blake's car were gone. The yellow station wagon she had observed upon arriving had also departed, indicating that it belonged to Jeb Fulmer and the black van to Griffith. As if reading her mind, he stood beside it. "Do you need a ride back to your office? I'd be happy to drive you."

"I'll hitch a lift with the crime scene boys," she said with a nod toward their small gray panel truck.

Griffith ran a hand across the black van's gleaming hood. "I bought a four-wheel drive because it seemed right for my new role as a country squire," he said bitterly. "Maybe if I had stayed in the city, Jonathan would still be alive."

"Excuse me, Mr. Griffith," she replied sharply. "That is a ridiculously maudlin way of looking at this. If Jonathan Dodge was going to be murdered, he would have been, regardless of where you happened to live."

"I can't help asking myself, 'Why was he here? Why didn't h
tell me he was coming?' "

"When we find out who killed him, we may learn answers to
those questions as well."

The coroner's wagon began moving slowly under the canopy of
trees along the driveway.

"I read in some mystery novel a long time ago that the job of the
detective is to add two and two and make it equal six," Griffith said
as the wagon vanished into deep shadows. "But none of this adds
up to me. I guess that just proves that real murder is a lot different
than I make it out to be in the yarns I knit. Jonathan used to rib me
mercilessly for being a romantic and for turning a murder story into
a morality lesson. He said morality had nothing to do with murder.
He believed everyone was capable of it and the only reason everyone didn't turn to murder was fear. The fear of being caught. He
meant premeditated murder, not heat-of-passion homicide. He'd
find it ironic and pretty funny if it should turn out that I write the
book on his murder."

"If it is a murder."

"Come now, Miss Flynn. *I* know it. *You* know it. It's as obvious
as two and two adding up to . . ."

Winning little crow's-feet formed at the corners of her eyes as
she laughed. "I know. Six."

12

Nuts About Mysteries

WHEN ARLENE FLYNN strode into his office, District Attorney Aaron Benson studied her above the rims of half-moon glasses. "Well, have you cracked this case yet?"

"It doesn't become a case until Zeligman says it is," she said, plopping wearily into a chair in front of his fastidious desk. In crossing her legs at the ankles, she revealed mud caked on the soles of her boots and the cuffs of her trousers. "God knows when we'll hear from him. They don't call him Herr Dr. Plodder for no reason."

"What's the story on the new owner of Traitor's Lair? Shall I draw up an arrest warrant?"

Brushing back a wayward strand of hair, she cracked a smile. "He wants to be my Dr. Watson."

Benson adjusted his glasses. "I beg your pardon?"

"His oldest friend in the world has yet to be slit open by Dr. Plodder in search of the cause of death, and Mr. Morgan Griffith, Es-*quire,* is already planning the true, inside story, soon-to-be-a-major-motion-picture or maybe a four-part TV mini-series book. He's asked me if he can be kept apprised of every development. I said I'd ask you."

Benson whipped off the glasses. "Screw that idea."

"Not so hasty, boss. Griffith could be an asset. He's more than eager to supply us with the names, addresses, phone numbers, and motives of plenty of suspects. It seems that Jonathan Dodge could never have been nominated for the Mr. Congeniality Award of the Mystery Writers of America, if there is such a thing. According to Griffith, Dodge put on quite a show at that organization's dinner

Friday night. Apparently, he pissed off every mystery nut in the place. Griffith told me, and I quote him almost verbatim, 'The way Jonathan was behaving, murdering him probably crossed everyone's mind.' "

Benson nodded. "That's *very* interesting."

"He cited two exceptions."

Benson rested his square chin on steepled fingers. "Who?"

"Chief of Detectives Harvey Goldstein. . . ."

"Goldstein?" Benson rocked in his chair, folded his hands on his belly, and laughed. "Harvey was at that soirée?"

"Along with a Sergeant John Bogdanovic."

"That's his assistant. They're a matched set. Bogdanovic is a brilliant detective. He's Goldstein twenty years ago. Yes, it makes sense that Harvey would be there. He's been nuts for mystery books and movies and the like for as long as I've known him, which is quite a few years. When I cut my prosecutorial teeth as a lowly assistant in the Manhattan D.A.'s Office, Harvey was an inspector and head of the Homicide Bureau. He was always harassing me to read detective novels so I'd appreciate what he called the art of murder. If this turns out to be a homicide, you and I should expect Harvey to try to grab jurisdiction."

Flynn bolted up. "Not a chance. The body was found here."

"It was *dumped* here. We don't know where the hell he died," Benson said, flattening his hands on the tidy desktop. "If we do determine Dodge was actually murdered in the city, our brothers in crime down there are going to want to take over. But in any event, I'm going to have to give Goldstein a call, in case you'll need the assistance of his office as you conduct your inquiries. If it develops there is a murder case to be prosecuted, I'll arm wrestle for who gets the honor with the Manhattan D.A. For now, what does your gut instinct tell you about where it happened?"

She frowned. "I'd bet in the city."

"Why haul the corpse all the way up here when New York's got two very accommodating rivers, scads of vacant lots and abandoned buildings up the kazoo?"

"Griffith suggested it was placed on his property by someone who wanted to point the finger of suspicion at him."

"Was he specific as to whom? And why?"

"The only name he mentioned in terms of being a suspect was Guido Perillo."

The district attorney shook his head incredulously. "Why in hell would an underworld boss bother to kill an author?"

"According to Griffith, Dodge's new book coming out in the fall is a biography of Perillo. Quite unflattering, I presume."

"If someone were writing a book about me that I didn't want published and I were the Godfather of organized crime, I'd have him killed *before* he wrote it. And why would he have the body dumped at Traitor's Lair? Why not in some swamp in the Jersey Meadowlands? The location of the body bothers me."

"Griffith says all his friends knew he bought the property. So let's suppose that one of them had it in for both Dodge and Griffith. Kill one, put the other on the spot."

"Are you proposing Dodge was elected simply because it was Griffith who had the place in the country?"

"There's another motive suggested during the fireside chat I had with Griffith. Dodge was gay. He had a live-in lover by the name of Jimmy something. They might have had a domestic tiff. We can't discount the possibility that one of the games that boys play went awry."

Benson frowned. "Well, until we get Zeligman's verdict, it's all speculation, isn't it? It's also a Sunday afternoon. A *late* Sunday afternoon. There's nothing for you to do here, Arlene. Go home and relax. Get your mind off murder. Watch a little TV."

"Obviously, you don't watch it much. Sunday is J. B. Fletcher night on the tube."

Benson looked blank. "I'm sorry. I never heard of him."

Flynn strode toward the door with her gun-heavy bag slung over her shoulder. "Not him," she said, pausing. "*Jessica* Fletcher is an author of mystery novels who figures out who done it on a show called *Murder, She Wrote*. If your friend Chief Goldstein is as nuts about mysteries as you say, I'll wager he never misses it."

"That's TV for you. A woman who solves crimes!" He clucked his tongue. "What *will* they dream up next?"

13

Mystery in the Air

ALTHOUGH THE HOUSE she had left early that morning had been painstakingly furnished, perhaps overly so, Flynn opened the door to a feeling of emptiness as real as the hauntingly vacant rooms of Traitor's Lair.

Dropping her bag on a table placed next to the front door specifically for that purpose, she thought about the woman who worked for the district attorney on Griffith's favorite boyhood radio program, and pictured Miss Miller arriving home each evening from work to a nest as quiet and empty as her own. Everyone who tuned in to "Mr. District Attorney" knew that because she was *Miss* Miller it was impermissible in the America of the 1930s and 1940s for her to find a lover, even in the big, sophisticated city of a county whose citizens the boss she called "Chief" had sworn himself to protect.

That Griffith had been able to recite the words of the oath he had heard again and again on the radio as a boy had stirred a feeling of fondness in her, not for a man whom she had to regard as a murder suspect, though she doubted he had killed Dodge, but for the child he had been in a country before it lost its innocence. He had known an America that her contemporaries in the 1960s disdained with callow arrogance.

When she chose to become a police officer at a point when all cops were pigs, she felt their scathing rejection as well. Yet Flynn had never regretted her choice, even when confronted at the end of a day's work with empty rooms and an evening to be spent alone either with work brought home from the office, a new book to read, or before the television screen in hope of finding a crime mystery whose solution she did not discern in the first few minutes, or which did not end leaving her feeling cheated.

To critics of crime shows who contended they constituted a bad influence on youth, Flynn answered that in all the cases the criminals got what was coming to them, for, as the Shadow had warned Morgan Griffith's generation on the radio every week, "The weed of crime bears bitter fruit. Crime does not pay."

That mystery and detective programs promulgated this truth had been the theme of her college thesis. "Through seven decades mystery, murder, and mayhem have been a staple of the air waves," she had written in the introduction, "and the persistent message conveyed has been that the law and justice will always prevail."

Since the first program with crime as a theme went on the air in 1930, there had been no less than five hundred series, amounting to tens of thousands of hours of chilling listening and viewing. Television alone offered more than three hundred series since 1948. Obviously, Americans loved them. Into their living rooms and hearts they had taken Charlie Chan, the Thin Man, the Shadow, Martin Kane, the monotone cops of Jack Webb's *Dragnet,* Columbo, the uniformed cops of the Pittsburgh Hill Street precinct, the plainclothes detectives working the streets of San Francisco, the New York faces and accents of *Naked City, Kojak,* and *Law and Order,* and the cops of Baltimore on *Homicide: Life on the Streets.*

When official police could not quench the thirst for sleuths, there were private eyes, from Sam Spade to Magnum. And lest an innocent person be punished, the wrongfully accused could always turn to Perry Mason.

During World War II and the Cold War, a brigade of secret agents and spies filled the need for adventure and mystery. For who were the daring and wordly figures such as James Bond and George Smiley at their core but gumshoe detectives?

But if American-style crime and punishment did not satisfy, there was murder most English, from Sherlock Holmes in Victorian times to the brutal realities of 1990s London's Detective Chief Inspector Jane Tennison.

Despite Flynn's remark to Benson that Sunday night belonged to Jessica Fletcher, the program starring Angela Lansbury was not her favorite when she tuned in for mystery. She preferred the kindred solitariness of Inspector Morse of the Oxford Constabulary—

his mind, his shared love of classical music, and the doggedness. Setting the control pads of her kitchen's microwave stove to provide a complete, nutritious hot dinner in the six minutes she intended to spend in the shower washing off the mud and grime of Traitor's Lair, she asked aloud, "What would Morse make of the body in the boathouse?"

Later, sitting before the TV set with the microwaved meal on a TV tray in her lap, she waited for *Murder, She Wrote* to come on. Presently, as always, Jessica unmasked the real murderer and explained to the police how he had done it and why, still leaving ample time for two more commercials, a hug and a laugh with the youth her sleuthing had saved from a life in prison, the rolling of the credits, and a plug for the following program.

Flynn went to bed realizing she had one other commonality with Inspector Morse. He also suffered from a cantankerous medical examiner who took his own damn time.

AT SIX IN THE MORNING, the ringing of her phone jolted her from a dream about lions.

"Good, you're up," growled the gruff voice. "It's Plodder. That tidy corpse of yours kept me up all night. It really bugged the hell out of me. It still does. How soon can you come see me?"

With an incredulous glance at her bedside clock, she said, "I'll be there in fifteen minutes."

"Good. Stop at that doughnut place on the way and pick me up a couple of jellies and a coffee, black with sugar on the side, and whatever you'd like for yourself. I'm buying."

14

Death Speaks

IN SIDE-BY-SIDE black frames on the wall behind his desk in the basement mortuary of Stone County Medical Center, Dr. Zeligman displayed two verities of his trade. On the left as you faced the desk was a quote from the Book of Job:

HE DISCOVERETH DEEP THINGS OUT OF DARKNESS,
AND BRINGETH OUT TO LIGHT THE SHADOW OF DEATH.

The other copied the inscription on the wall of the medical examiner's office in New York City:

THIS IS THE PLACE WHERE DEATH
DELIGHTS TO HELP THE LIVING.

In a row below ran similarly framed drawings of indelible moments and portraits of significant contributors to the history of forensic pathology. Arranged chronologically left to right were the third-century B.C. Alexandrian physicians Erasistratus and Herophilus, who conducted the first postmortem examinations, though not in the pursuit of murder; an artist's imagined portrait of the Roman physician who analyzed the stab wounds in the body of Julius Caesar and declared that of the twenty-three, only one to the heart had proved fatal; the first-century A.D. Greco-Roman physician Galen, whose studies of gladiators became a landmark in the study of human anatomy; unknown Chinese medical examiners of the thirteenth century whose work resulted in publication of the *Hsi Yuan Lu,* a codification of studies of the means of death in murder victims; the Flemish anatomist and dissectionist Andreas Vesalius; Ambroise Paré, Paolo Zacchia, and Fortunato Fidelis, all of whom contributed to the knowledge of homicidal wounds; Giovanni Battista, scrupulous recorder of postmortems; Johann Franck, a proponent of physicians treating legal medicine as seriously as their clinical practice; the legendary Sir Bernard Spilsbury of England, whose laboratory genius was matched by his abilities to dispel the mysteries of murder in a courtroom in such celebrated cases as wife-murderer Dr. Hawley Harvey Crippen, George Joseph Smith of the "Brides in the Bath" murders, dismemberment murderer Patrick Mahon, and the Brighton trunk murders; James S. Stringham, first Professor of Medical Jurisprudence in the United States; and the three giants of American forensic medicine: Alan Moritz, Michael Baden, and Milton Helpern, who had installed in the New York City Morgue the second truth framed behind Theodore Zeligman's desk.

Rumpled and red-eyed, the doctor clutched a paper cup of coffee in encircling hands as if he were a celebrant of the mass handling the chalice of wine transsubstantiated to the Blood of Christ.

"I was going to let this murder case of yours go until this afternoon or evening," he said. "But its uniqueness kept gnawing at me. I couldn't let it slide. I needed to satisfy myself as to cause of death."

"You said 'murder.' "

"Oh, he was murdered," Zeligman said, setting aside the cup. "I am satisfied that the man did not die where he was found. I am satisfied that he died sitting up but with his head tilted back, as if he were sleeping upright as people do on airplanes. I have slept that way myself many times after dozing off in my favorite armchair following a big meal or watching TV. I am satisfied that the body was moved shortly after death and laid on its back. I am satisfied that it was then handled somewhat roughly while it was being transported to the place where it was discovered."

"What about cause of death?"

"I'm satisfied that he did not die of strangulation, of poisoning, of stabbing or cutting, or by being shot in the torso. I am also satisfied that death was the result of massive intracranial hemorrhaging. It's the cause of that bleeding which has left me mystified. When you encounter such a condition, three possible causes present themselves. First, in a man of this individual's age, you would look for stroke. Number two: a trauma to the head from a blow. Three: a bullet in the brain. Well, this man did not suffer a stroke. Nor is there evidence of his being struck, either by an instrument or a fist. That leaves the third possibility."

"A gunshot."

"But this is what has bugged me all night. You must look at the X-rays. Come into the autopsy room."

Two bodies covered by heavy rubber sheets lay on high steel tables at the center of a large, brightly lit room kept so cold that Flynn shivered as she entered. Following the medical examiner, she came to a long row of rectangular opaque glass screens mounted on a stainless steel wall. A click of a switch that seemed as loud as a gun being fired illuminated them. Zeligman deftly slid a large X-ray picture of a human skull under a pair of metal clips.

"This view is the right side of the head," he explained. "Others from the left side and at different angles show the same. You'll see a dark mass in the lower section of the skull. That's a large pooling of blood. Above that mass you'll find what appears to be a bullet path. Do you see it?"

"Yes I do," she said, as his stubby index finger traced a straight narrow white line from the mouth to the back of the head and above the beginning of the spinal cord.

"It begins in the soft tissues at the rear of the palate. I will show you in the roof of the man's mouth what appears to be a small entrance wound, if you wish. But first, make a note that the path passes through the lower portion to the brain stem and ends there." The finger stabbed the point. He stepped aside. "Do you see it clearly?"

"Yes, that's what it looks like."

Zeligman took her arm and drew her closer. "Now tell me what you *don't* see."

Tugging her lower lip, Flynn repeated, "What I don't see?"

He tapped the X-ray with a fist. "Where is the bullet?"

She shrugged. "It must have exited."

Zeligman shook his head slowly. "I'm sorry. It did *not* exit. There . . . is . . . no . . . exit . . . wound. I will show you the body. Nor did it fragment. There are no fragments in any of the X-rays.

Yet I have found *no bullet*. So you tell me. Where is this fatal bullet? Was this bullet made of some magical metal?"

"I read a story once in which there was a bullet made of ice and it melted in the wound," Flynn said, feeling foolish even as she spoke. "Or maybe it was a movie. Ridiculous, huh?"

"Bah! Fiction writers! Melting bullet—such utter nonsense! There can be only one explanation. There is no bullet because he was not shot. The small wound in the mouth is not the entrance wound of a bullet. It's a puncture wound."

Her eyes went wide. "Are you telling me this man was stabbed in the mouth with an instrument that penetrated all the way into the back of his brain?"

"That is the only explanation."

"What could possibly do that?"

"How about an ice pick?"

She made a face. "Who uses an ice pick these days?"

"My late wife had a hatpin that was certainly long enough to inflict just such a deep wound."

"I'm afraid women's hats are out of fashion, Doctor. And the hatpin has gone the way of the whalebone corset."

"A stiletto would do. Or have they gone out of fashion?"

"If you have a stiletto at hand to kill someone, why not just slit the throat?"

"Now you force me to conjecture, which is your job. But a slit throat produces a great deal of spurting blood. So does the stabbing of the body. Both would require a great deal of cleaning up. People who kill by stabbing or cutting of throats also are likely to leave their victims in place. But a stab wound that penetrates deeply in the brain would result in far less bleeding. Death would be virtually instantaneous. Whatever bleeding might occur would be contained within the skull. And with the head in a backward-tilted position as this man's was at time of death, the blood would pool in a kind of natural bowl, as it did in this instance. Very, very tidy."

"The scenario you've sketched is this. Dodge was stabbed in the mouth so deeply that the wound caused massive bleeding in the brain, which killed him instantly. He was seated at the time, his head tilted back. Right?"

"Correct."

"Would you say he was conscious?"

"I can say that he had not been rendered unconscious by a blow of any sort. There are no bruises, abrasions, or contusions anywhere on the body. But I cannot tell you if he was conscious."

"You found no indication that he struggled?"

"None."

"Could he have been tied up?"

"There are no signs of it. There's no welting of wrists or ankles, as you might expect if someone were trussed up with rope or a belt, for instance."

"What can you tell me about possible sexual activity around the time of death?"

"Are you asking if he might have been engaging in some kind of sadomasochistic activity?"

"I guess I am."

"I can state with reasonable certitude that Mr. Dodge had recently engaged in the receptive role during anal intercourse."

"How recently?"

"Some hours before death."

"By the way, what was the time of death?"

"I cannot be more specific now than late Friday night or early Saturday morning."

"Do you have any idea whether he was clothed at the time of his death?"

"This answer is not based on science, but experience. The man was clothed in a tuxedo. Having had to dress myself in one from time to time, I can tell you that it is never an easy task. To put one on a corpse would be, I think, a very difficult job. Unless you happen to be a funeral director. And even they have tricks to make clothing bodies easier."

"One other thing, Doctor. Had he been drinking?"

"The blood alcohol level was highly elevated."

"Was he drunk?"

"That's a subjective word. He had consumed a large amount of alcohol. Considering the tuxedo, I'd guess he had been at a party of some kind. Is that a reasonable deduction?"

"You're right on the money, Doctor. He was Guest of Honor."

PART FOUR

Accomplices in Crime

A trusty comrade is always of use.

—SHERLOCK HOLMES

15

At Your Service

CHIEF OF DETECTIVES Harvey Goldstein toyed with a strand of sparse brown hair, teasing it and curling it around a finger and leaving Arlene Flynn to wonder as she watched if the unconscious habit might have contributed to his baldness.

"As I promised your boss and my old friend Aaron Benson on the telephone yesterday, Miss Flynn," he said, "the facilities of the New York Police Department are at your service. And I've put my own assistant at your disposal."

His eyes turned to a lanky young man in a brown tweed coat and charcoal slacks slouched in a soft black leather armchair to her right.

"When it comes to homicide, you won't find a better detective than Johnny Bogdanovic. If you don't believe me, ask *him.*"

As Bogdanovic came up straight, he smiled like one who had abided the joke many times and asked, "Where would you like to start, Miss Flynn?"

"Since we're to be accomplices in crime, how about beginning with you calling me Arlene and I'll call you John?"

"You can call him anything," said Goldstein, "except late for dinner."

Bogdanovic winced.

"On the subject of food," she said, "I'm informed that by coincidence you two were guests at the Mystery Writers of America dinner Friday evening. That appears to have been the last time Jonathan Dodge was seen alive. Except by his murderer."

Bogdanovic crossed his legs and jiggled a loafered foot. "He was lucky nobody killed him then and there. The guy apparently had made more enemies than anyone since Nixon was in the White House. Frankly, I didn't care much for him myself."

"Why not?"

"He was arrogant, sarcastic, bullying, smug, and vain. You should have seen the cape he had on. And the fancy cane."

"Did he have a physical impairment?"

"Cane's the wrong word," Goldstein said. "Dodge carried a gentleman's walking stick. A hell of a nice one, too. Its top was a little Maltese Falcon in silver. I thought it was appropriate for the occasion."

"There was no walking stick found with the body."

Bogdanovic placed both feet flat on the floor and drummed his fingers on the arm of his chair. "Shall we check the files for killers who collect walking sticks?"

"There was no cape at the scene, either. Does the New York Police Department have a file on people with cape fetishes?"

"That'll teach you to joke about murder," Goldstein jibed.

"You didn't mind the joking that was going on at our table Friday night," Bogdanovic replied sulkily.

Goldstein smiled benignly. "I think you'd better put your new partner in the picture, John."

Bogdanovic lurched forward eagerly. "Everybody at our table took great delight in plotting how to bump Dodge off, either together or singly. Then they passed it off as a big joke on me." He sank back. "I wonder if they're laughing now."

"Do you recall who took part in their macabre humor?"

"If I can't, all the guests were listed table by table in the evening's program."

"I've kept mine as a souvenir," Goldstein said.

"Did anyone strike either of you as being more capable of murder than another?"

"They all sounded pretty bloodthirsty to me," Bogdanovic said, slouching again.

"Chief, would you care to suggest a suspect?"

"To borrow a mystery-writing cliché, 'I suspect everyone.' Aside from the guest list, how would you like to proceed with your investigation?"

"I'm going to need to look around Dodge's home. Even though

I believe I have probable cause to go inside without a warrant, I thought it might be prudent to get one. I understand Dodge had a young man living with him. I want to be prepared in the event he might object to police snooping around."

"I'll handle that," said Goldstein. "It won't take long. How do you intend to get in, should no one be at home?"

"A key recovered from the body appears to be to the house."

"What's being done with the rest of the evidence recovered at the scene?"

"It's been forwarded to the state police crime lab."

"At some point you might think about letting our lab people go over it as well."

"Thank you. Meanwhile, I'm going to have another chat with the man on whose property the body was found. He was Dodge's best friend. I'd like to learn more from him about Dodge's life."

" 'I shall know the murderer when I know the victim well.' The gospel of homicide investigation, according to Georges Simenon's Inspector Jules Maigret. Are you a reader of crime fiction, Arlene? If not, I heartily recommend you become one. I find there is always something in them to educate me. Who is it you'll be seeing today?"

"His name is Morgan Griffith."

"Ah, yes, I remember him," said Bogdanovic. "He and Dodge crossed swords over cocktails before the dinner."

"He's got an apartment on the Upper West Side. Number 340, West Eighty-ninth Street," she said, lifting her handbag off the floor. "What's the parking situation likely to be around there?"

"We'll take the Chief's car," Bogdanovic answered, rising smoothly out of the deep chair. "It's got a little card in the window to shoo away any traffic enforcement officers and their tow trucks. Where are you parked now?"

"On a public lot a few blocks west."

"Next time put it in our garage downstairs," Goldstein said. "I'll arrange that for you, too. I should have your warrant after lunch."

"People think the mayor runs this town," Bogdanovic said. "They're wrong. Mayors come and go. Goldstein rules forever."

"If this man gets out of line in any way, Arlene, you let me know," Goldstein said, picking up a phone to arrange the warrant and the parking. "Johnny, you keep in touch. I don't want my old pal the D.A. of Stone County calling up for a progress report and catching the Chief of Detectives with his pants down."

. Leaving the office with Bogdanovic, Flynn wondered if Goldstein's order to him might have been the first step in attempting to take over the case. But as they stepped into the elevator, Bogdanovic said, "You're worried that we're going to move in on your investigation, aren't you?"

She looked at him astonished. "Whatever gave you that idea?"

"Being a cop, I know how they think. It's what I'd be worrying about if the tables were turned. I assure you that neither Chief Goldstein nor I have any interest in elbowing you and your boss aside. We've got enough murder cases to clear to last us into the next century, and new ones every day. So, as far as we're concerned, the lead investigator in this case is Arlene Flynn."

"I never doubted it."

"I must say I like your style, Arlene."

"As the saying goes, 'You ain't seen nothin' yet.' "

"Of course, if it turns out Dodge *was* murdered in New York City, it will have to become our case. That's the law. I'm sure you recognize that."

"All that matters in the end is making an arrest and putting together the evidence that will result in a conviction. I'm sure *you* recognize that. Now let's leave the politics for another day and solve the murder of Jonathan Dodge, no matter where it took place. Okay?"

He saluted her crisply. "At your service, boss."

16

Guest List

"SO WHAT'S YOUR THEORY?" Bogdanovic asked as he drove from the garage. "And please don't tell me you haven't formed one because there is insufficient data to go on, or your mind's wide open."

"Before I show you mine, you must show me yours," she said. "After all, you do have me at a disadvantage. You were a guest at that dinner. I think we must assume that you broke bread with the murderer. Whom do you nominate as prime suspect?"

"How about the guy who found the body?"

"The body was discovered by a local contractor. Jeb Fulmer."

"You know who I mean. Griffith."

"That dog doesn't hunt. If Griffith did it, why wouldn't he shove the body in the Hudson and let it float away down into your jurisdiction? Why would Griffith choose to murder Dodge on his own property in the first place? And why leave the body in a boathouse Fulmer had been hired to tear down that weekend?"

"Maybe he forgot about Fulmer. Maybe it wasn't premeditated murder. How about an accident of some kind?"

"One does not die accidentally by way of something penetrating the brain through the mouth. Let's discount Griffith."

"All right. Applying the rule they seem to follow in movies and on TV shows that the killer is always the last one you would expect, the name that comes to my mind next is Elvira Eveland, a little old lady with a grip like iron."

"Was she wearing a hat held fast by a long pin?"

"Sorry. No hat."

"Anyway, a little old lady would have needed an accomplice to heft Dodge into that shack."

"Scratch Elvira from the list?"

After a brief silence as he negotiated the car into uptown traffic, she surprised him by looking at him sideways and asking, "How long were you in the Marine Corps?"

His smile formed crinkles at the corners of his mouth. "Who told you I was a Marine?"

"Nobody. You can always tell a Marine. Though not much."

"Old joke. And a lame one the first time I heard it."

"It's arithmetic. I figure that to get where you are in the NYPD you have to have been on the force at least ten years. I assume you were typical of those who are drawn to police work and signed up at the earliest age permitted. I know that the minimum required by the NYPD ten years ago was twenty-one. You certainly look to be at least thirty-one now; I think you're closer to thirty-five, actually. Figuring that you chose not to delay joining the force by attending college, I am left with a gap of approximately four years. I can't see you wasting them. What would you do? You would want to keep in shape. Gain some experience. That leaves the Marines."

"Why not the Army or Navy?"

"Instinct tells me you'd go for the service that boasts it's looking for a few good men. That would appeal to your vanity."

"*Vanity?*"

"Save the protest. Your clothing speaks volumes on the subject. You probably enlisted especially for whatever the Marines call their military police."

"I'm thirty-six, actually. When I went to join the police force, there was a hiring freeze. So, I did three years in the USMC as an M.P. When it came time to get out of the Corps, I discovered I would have to wait a couple of years before there would be a new class at the Police Academy. I reenlisted in the Corps for three years. As for you, I'm confident in saying that you took the academic route and had a very rough time of it once you got on the force, on account of being a woman, but by sheer guts, willpower, and brains you got to where you are today."

"Approximately correct."

"Approximately *hell*. Shall I elucidate the method by which I reached my conclusions?"

"Please do, Sherlock."

"When Chief Goldstein informed me I'd be the one to extend the courtesies of the NYPD to you, I called a newspaper guy I know who covers Stone County courts and got filled in on you."

"Name that dirty squealing rat."

"I never disclose a confidential source."

"Have you and your boss considered the likelihood that you and he could be called to the stand when the murderer of Jonathan Dodge comes to trial? I don't mean to testify as police officers. I refer to your being at that dinner Friday night. Might there be a conflict between being eyewitnesses to what went on then and your involvement in this investigation?"

"Everyone at the dinner knew who and what we were. I can't see anyone making a successful claim of infringement of constitutional rights against self-incrimination."

"How many people were there?"

"A couple of hundred. At my table, nine."

"Including Dodge?"

"As recipient of the big award of the night he was seated at Table One. With me at Table Two were Chief Goldstein, Griffith, Elvira Eveland, Margaret Tinney, Alexander Somerfield, an agent named Myron Frank, a combination portrait painter and author by the name of Vernon Ney, and an old friend of Chief Goldstein who goes only by the monicker Wiggins."

"Nine at a table. Isn't it customary to have an even number of chairs?"

"There was a tenth. It wasn't occupied."

"Do you know who the no-show was?"

"The name escapes me. It will be on the seating list in the program. Griffith may remember."

Swinging wide the door to his apartment on the top floor of a four-story brownstone, Griffith greeted them with, "It didn't take your coroner long to confirm the obvious, Miss Flynn. But the news story I heard on the radio this morning about Jonathan's murder omitted the cause of death. Would I be wrong in assuming that detail was purposely kept from the press?"

Breathless after the steep climb, she muttered, "Assume anything you like, Mr. Griffith."

"I'm sorry. That assumption was the unreconstructed newsman

in me talking. Not to mention the Sherlockian. It was Holmes who told Watson that the press is a most valuable institution if you know how to use it. Come into the living room." Turning to Bogdanovic, he smiled and said, "Nice to see you again, Sergeant B."

"Likewise, Mr. Griffith."

"I can't say that I'm surprised you've also turned up at my door. I figured Miss Flynn's investigation would have to come to the city sooner or later. Professional courtesy would dictate at least a nod in the direction of the NYPD. And because you and your boss had been among those who were the last to see Jonathan alive, the Chief of Detectives would not take a passive role in the case. Who else could he assign but you? Pardon the mess. I'm in the process of moving a lot of my stuff to my country place. God, doesn't that sound pretentious? *Country place.*"

Flynn paused in the doorway to a large, sunny room with walls covered by the artifacts of Griffith's life, career, and passions. Immediately to her left a glass cabinet displayed the awards and trophies of journalistic achievement, surrounded by a photo exhibit of him with newsmakers going back four decades.

"You told me your friends called your apartment a museum. Now I see why," she said, studying a display of pictures of him against a variety of exotic backgrounds. In Moscow's Red Square, spires of old churches with tops like onions loomed behind him as he stood side by side with Dodge, both looking like misplaced capitalists. A narrow alley that appeared to be in the Middle East found them in short-sleeved khaki shirts, wearing black-and-white-checkered scarves she had seen Arabs wearing on television newscasts. Backed by a street full of Asian faces, he smoked a pipe between Dodge and a third man with a cigarette. "Where was this?"

"Saigon. My first assignment there in 1966. Jonathan and the guy with us, Gene Valentine, had been in the country a year by then. If I look scared to death it's because I was. Good God, it seems like a century ago. Now Jonathan's dead, Lord knows where Gene is these days, and Saigon is Ho Chi Minh City. That's life, huh?"

"Life is going on with living, and you know it." She stepped sideways to a row of bookcases. "You have quite a library."

"If you want to write, you have to read. I'm in the process of deciding which books stay here and which will go to Traitor's Lair. Occasionally, I wonder if it might make more sense to haul them down to the Strand bookstore, sell 'em, and start over."

Examining leatherbound editions of his books, she asked, "How many novels have you written?"

"If you're asking how many I've had published, the number is twenty-two. I've written a few more that were deemed unsuitable for publication. Wisely so, in retrospect."

Below his works stretched a shelf of Jonathan Dodge titles, also morocco-bound. "Are these all the books he wrote?"

"A complete set, arranged chronologically, as are mine. He always presented me with a specially bound copy of his latest and I did the same. I enjoyed ribbing him about him getting the better deal. He countered with the fact that he might have written fewer but they were thicker than mine. He also pointed out that all I had to do was sit down and make up stuff, whereas he was writing about real events and therefore had the much harder job. Have you read any of his works?"

"This and this," she said, tapping volumes dealing with the Boston Strangler and Son of Sam. "Which of the others would you recommend? You mentioned one concerning a detective trying to track down a murderer during wartime. It sounded interesting."

"That's the third of his books," Griffith said, drawing it from the shelf. *Incident on Tu Do Street,* 1970. Jonathan did much better writing after this one. The Son of Sam book in 1978 was excellent. But the work I liked the best was *Secrets of Lubyanka.* It came out last October and dipped into my specialty before the demise of the Soviet Union and the ending of the Cold War pretty much spelled the end to the James Bond/George Smiley genre. Fortunately, by then I'd chosen not to put all my eggs in that golden goose's basket and added a line of hard-boiled whodunits to my repertoire. Critics took me to task for it, advising me to return to the territory I had explored in *Echoes from the Woods.* I'm glad I didn't heed their advice. But getting back to Jonathan. His best work isn't out yet. That's the book on Guido Perillo that I mentioned. I've got the galleys. If you think they might help you, I can dig them out of this mess."

Bogdanovic sidled up next to him. "Could Perillo have gotten a set of galleys?"

"If you have contacts in publishing or the printing trades, they're easy to obtain. I can usually get my hands on a set if a book interests me."

Bogdanovic drifted to shelves displaying a Sherlock Holmes collection almost as vast as the one in Wiggins's office.

"This must be a unique experience for you, Sergeant B, to have met not only the victim but all the likely suspects on the same occasion," Griffith said. "Indeed, only a few hours before the murder, if, as seems likely, Jonathan met his death soon after the MWA dinner."

"Was that the only time you saw him?" Flynn asked. "Did you see him after the dinner? Getting into a taxi? Do you remember if you saw Dodge with anyone in particular after the dinner?"

"I'd *expected* to see him for drinks at a reception that's held every year at the Usual Suspects bookstore by the owner. You were there, too, Sergeant, along with Chief Goldstein."

"It was a very nice party."

"So you know that when Jonathan didn't show up, Wiggins was really put out about it. That was the first time in the fifteen years Wiggins has been offering brandy and cigars that the Grand Master recipient didn't show up. Now we know why."

Bogdanovic turned from Sherlock Holmes to a wall festooned with a collection of political buttons. "Do we?"

"Isn't it reasonable to assume Jonathan didn't come to the reception because he'd already been murdered or was in the process of being?"

"I figured he didn't come because he'd made such an ass of himself about Wiggins passing himself off with a phony name and threatening to dig up the proof in London."

"That's a fool's errand, Sergeant. Everyone who knows good old Wiggins presumes his name is an affectation. The only thing Jonathan could achieve by proving it's a pseudonym would be to embellish Wiggins's reputation as a likable rogue."

"Does that include peddling fake first editions?"

"Now you're getting into a very gray area."

Bogdanovic's attention diverted to a glass display case containing cast-metal miniatures of famous ocean liners, then returned to Griffith. "Was there anyone Dodge did not offend or pick a fight with at the dinner?"

"There must have been someone in the hundreds who attended the dinner. But of those closest to him, probably not. Jonathan was in rare form that night. He seemed to ooze venom from every gland and spray it in all directions. You listened to his speech accepting the Grand Master award."

"For the benefit of one who wasn't there," Flynn said, "what did he say?"

"I can only give you the gist. But there's a recording of it. Oscar Pendleton always arranges for the Edgar presentations to be taped. Oscar's big on history. He also publishes a collection of the remarks, updating it every few years."

"The gist will do for the moment."

"He spent fifteen minutes taking the hide off the entire publishing establishment. Not enough advertising and promotion. Treating authors like peons. Editors who are so loaded with books to get out that they don't have time to edit. Turning the editing process over to literary agents, many of whom he accused of being more agent than literary. Questionable accounting methods. Questionable earnings statements. The near extinction of the independent publishing house. Mergers and takeovers by bottom-line Wall Streeters who nurture no regard for literature or those who produce it. An industry mired in the nineteenth century. And critics who write long essays in the *Sunday Times* book section that seem longer than the books they're purportedly reviewing. Who imagined we were listening to Jonathan's swan song?"

"Obviously someone imagined it," Bogdanovic replied. "Our entire table made sport of the prospect of ridding the publishing world of his presence. Elvira Eveland was especially upset after talking with Dodge before we sat down for dinner."

"Can you honestly envision little old Elvira Eveland killing anyone? Especially a big guy like Jonathan?"

"With a little help from her friends, why not?"

"Such as Maggie Tinney? She's so frail a sneeze in her direction would blow her into the middle of next week."

"There was nothing frail about that artist at our table."

"I concede that Vernon Ney possesses the physique required to tote Jonathan down a hill and into my boathouse at night and in the mud, but why should he?"

"What's the story about Dodge having cheated Ney out of his fee for a portrait? And something about a slander suit?"

"Jonathan was a lot like the character in *The Hound of the Baskervilles* who enjoyed finding cause to take people to court. He thought Ney's interpretation of the subject insulted him."

"What was your opinion of the picture?" Flynn asked.

"I liked it. I told Jonathan he was being foolish. I said to him that if he hated it, he ought to do what Winston Churchill did with a portrait he'd despised. He took it home and secretly got rid of it. Alternatively, I suggested he could stick it in the attic à la Dorian Gray and hope that all his sins would transfer themselves from his heart to the painting's. I believe what Jonathan hoped to achieve by way of the lawsuit was to compel Vern Ney to destroy the picture himself, probably in public."

"In other words, he wanted to humiliate the artist," Bogdanovic said with a look of disgust. "The way he humiliated Elvira Eveland by dragging her away for some mysterious reason that left the poor woman shaken and white as a ghost. The way he humiliated everyone that night."

Griffith replied with a shrug, "I told Miss Flynn that Jonathan was not a very nice man."

"How did he treat you?"

"As badly as everyone else. But for a much longer period of time, of course. Jonathan was my oldest friend. That's why, if you're thinking I killed him—which I'm sure you are—I tell you that I did not murder him. Believe me, over the years of our relationship he'd given me plenty of cause. I had countless opportunities. I could have left him dead in Vietnam, the Middle East, or in some alley in Communist Berlin. Well, I didn't then and I didn't on Friday night. In spite of everything awful I could tell you about Jonathan, I liked him. I admired him. And, yes, I even envied him."

"What was the nature of the bad blood between Dodge and his agent? That is, his former agent," Bogdanovic asked.

"The reason behind Jonathan severing his relationship with

Myron Frank was not disclosed by either of them. Maybe now that Jonathan's dead, Myron will feel free to explain. You'll have to ask Myron. I can give you his home address. I've got addresses and numbers for everyone who was at Table Two. The MWA publishes a membership list."

"Thanks. We'll manage. By the way, who was supposed to be the tenth guest at Table Two?"

"Harry Houdini."

Flynn jerked with surprise. "I beg your pardon? I thought Harry Houdini was dead and gone decades ago."

Griffith laughed. "I'm sorry. I spoke from force of habit. Everyone who knows Jack Bohannon automatically calls him by the name of the world's most famous magician. Jack is probably *the* expert on Houdini. He earned an Edgar a few years ago for the definitive biography. Jack was the right author to do it. He's an astonishing illusionist. He does an amazing trick with a sword."

"Maybe the tenth chair at Table Two wasn't vacant after all," Bogdanovic jibed. "Bohannon could have turned himself invisible for the night."

Flynn shot him a rebuking glance.

"If anyone could," Griffith said blithely, "it'd be Jack."

"Regarding those who were at Table Two," Bogdanovic said, "do you know why Dodge quit writing for his publisher? What was his name?"

"Oscar Pendleton. I'm sure it was because Jonathan could get more money with another house. It was a situation in which the author outgrew the firm that first published him. Jonathan had been thinking about it a long time. It's not a unique thing in the book trade these days. Of course, that was very little consolation for Oscar. He can no longer rely on the huge earnings from Jonathan's blockbusters to finance smaller books that Oscar enjoys publishing but could never recoup on the advances. Good old Oscar is of the old school. He's published many a book for no other reason than they deserved to be."

"There was one guest at Table Two who remained quiet through all the gossiping and griping about Dodge. An older man. White hair. Very distinguished looking."

"That was Alexander Somerfield. Alex is habitually quiet.

Before he retired and turned a hand to writing detective stories, he was a genuine intelligence agent. Jonathan and I have known him for years, going all the way back to the deepest freezes of the Cold War. Alex's cover was journalism. But we saw through it. I borrowed freely from what I knew about Alex when I created the main character in the espionage thrillers I used to crank out. Whether Alex was CIA or in some other agency that played East-West games I have never been able to squeeze out of him. I prefer to think he has jotted it all down for an autobiography that will be sprung on the world—posthumously, naturally. For now, Alex lives on a magnificent yacht that he berths at the Seventy-ninth Street marina. How's that for keeping up one's romantic, swashbuckling image?"

"How did Somerfield and Dodge get along?" Flynn asked.

"Jonathan treated Alex deferentially. I think deep down he felt intimidated by Alex. Maybe even afraid."

"Why would he be afraid of him?" Bogdanovic asked.

"Don't let Alex's debonair Douglas Fairbanks demeanor deceive you, Sergeant B. He can be a downright dangerous guy. For the right cause, that is."

"How about for the right money?"

"I don't follow you."

"What does a former spy do when there's nobody left for him to spy on? How does an ex-agent keep up the payments on a yacht?"

"I hope I haven't misled you, Sergeant B. Please don't get the impression that Alex's boat is some extravagant oceangoing cruiser or anything like that. As yachts go, his is a modest one. Very snug and trim. It's not like the ships an Onassis or a Trump would have. It's got a couple of bunks below and a galley. Very nice for boating up the river on a Sunday afternoon. But to this landlubber, that's a yacht. Just as I think of Jonathan's house on Gramercy Park as a mansion, when what it is, really, is an ordinary Manhattan town house with an extraordinary address and, consequently, a very impressive price tag. Have you been there?"

"It's our next stop," Flynn said, moving toward the foyer. "Thanks for seeing us. I'm sorry we bothered you in the middle of your packing."

"No bother at all. As I said, I want to be as helpful as I can in your search for Jonathan's murderer." Griffith looked at her hopefully. "What's the status of the Watson to your Holmes idea? Have you talked it over with Mr. Benson?"

"He's mulling it," she said, entering the foyer.

Next to the door Bogdanovic observed an umbrella stand made of rich dark wood and bristling with walking sticks and canes, most topped by carved dogs' heads. Removing one, he said, "I gather you collect these, too."

"Jonathan got me started. He said he was determined to bring walking sticks back into fashion. He used to harangue me about there not being enough style in the world. Then one day he showed up here with a magnificent antique ebony stick with the head of a dog in gold. He called it the Hound of the Baskervilles. It's the one you're holding in your hand. I've been adding walking sticks to the clutter of my life ever since. Trouble is, I'm too self-conscious about going out in the streets swinging one, except when I'm out with Jonathan. He demands it. *Demanded* it. I'm sorry. I find it hard to speak of him in the past tense."

"He had a cane with him at the dinner."

"As I said, he always carried one."

"The top was a bird of some kind."

"The Maltese Falcon. Made of solid silver. That stick was his favorite. About Jonathan's house, Miss Flynn. I told you he had a live-in lover."

"Jimmy something."

"I looked him up in my address book. It's Jimmy Clements. He was also known in Jonathan's gay circle as Jimmy Climax."

Bogdanovic grunted, "Charming," and replaced the stick.

"Do you need a key to the house? I have one that Jonathan kept here as a spare in the event he lost his."

"Thanks, but we have the one that was found on the body."

When they reached the sidewalk, Bogdanovic said, "I presume you were thinking the same thing I was when Griffith described Alexander Somerfield's boat?"

"It certainly could be an explanation for how Dodge's body made its way up the Hudson and into Griffith's boathouse," Flynn said as they got into the car. "That fits Griffith's scenario that the body was dumped at Traitor's Lair by someone hoping to settle scores with two enemies at once by killing Dodge and focusing suspicion on Griffith. This certainly moves Somerfield to the top of our roster of Jonathan Dodge's intriguing friends and interesting enemies. Johnny, how extensive are your confidential sources inside outfits that Somerfield might have worked for in carrying out his intelligence activities?"

"I developed a few professional friendships among the task force that came together at the time of the World Trade Center bombing. And I know a couple of guys who started out infiltrating the anti-war movement in the 1960s and the terrorist activities of the 1980s, although they may be a little rusty in the hinges by now. Digging into Somerfield's past as a spy won't be easy. My experience with spooks is that they're as tight-lipped as a frigid virgin on her wedding night. If we're going to poke around in Somerfield's background, we face the age-old dilemma, 'How do you spy on a spy?' "

"I'm sure you'll find a way."

"Before we open that can of worms, I think we need to find out if Somerfield took his boat from the marina Friday night."

"Yes. We may be getting excited for no reason." She paused, then blurted, *"As tight-lipped as a frigid virgin on her wedding night?* Even Mickey Spillane wouldn't touch that metaphor."

17

The House on Gramercy Square

"FAMILIAR TERRITORY," Bogdanovic said as he found a space for the car at the corner of Third Avenue and Twentieth Street. "I learned the basics of being a cop in this neighborhood. The Police Academy is half a block from here. And a couple of years after I graduated I worked out of the Thirteenth Precinct, just down the street. Dodge's house is on Gramercy Park West, a one-block walk."

As if they were a couple out for a stroll, they passed on the north side of a neatly groomed park enclosed by a tall black-painted iron fence and encompassed by flagstone pavement dappled by sunlight filtering through lush trees.

"One of Manhattan's wealthiest neighborhoods, Gramercy had been created out of marshland that the Dutch settlers of New York called *Krom Moerasje,* meaning 'the little crooked swamp,'" Bogdanovic explained. "By 1692, the term had been transformed to 'Crommashie,' and over succeeding years into 'Gramercy.' Draining it in 1831, a real estate developer, Samuel B. Ruggles, envisioned building a fenced park patterned after squares he had studied in London. To ensure privacy, a golden key would be provided to the purchasers of the sixty-six surrounding lots. Between Third and Fourth avenues, the square caused Lexington Avenue to dead-end at Twenty-first Street on the north side and formed the beginning of Irving Place on the south. Originally lined by rows of brick town houses with spacious rooms and high windows, the square had witnessed the inroads of a few twentieth-century apartment buildings. One of these was No. 12, and in it in the early 1920s had dwelt a colorful crook who staged the biggest robbery in

American history, the 1919 stick-up of a mail truck, getting away with $2.5 million in cash and negotiable securities.

"His name was Gerald Chapman and he was a dandy dresser, known around town as the Count of Gramercy Square," Bogdanovic continued, pointing across the park to the house where Chapman had lived. "But in 1924 he made the mistake of killing a cop in a bungled burglary in Connecticut. That foolhardy deed got him declared 'Public Enemy Number One,' the first time anybody was so named in history. They hanged him in 1926."

Half a block north of the Chapman address, Jonathan Dodge's four-story red brick house rose sedately behind a narrow iron-fenced garden, its white front door reached by eight stone steps. When no one answered several rings of the doorbell, Flynn inserted the key taken from Dodge's pocket. The lock turned with a satisfying click. Opening the door, she entered a small foyer illuminated by four tear-shaped bulbs in a brass sconce. "Police. Search warrant," she shouted. "Anyone here?"

Unanswered, she turned right and entered a long, brightly lighted and lavishly furnished parlor. Immediately before her stood a red plush Victorian settee. Draped across its gracefully curved back was a blue opera cape. Laid over it was the walking stick with the handle in the shape of a silver bird.

"Obviously, Dodge came home after the dinner," Bogdanovic said. "The question now is whether this is where he was killed. Let's have a look around."

Proceeding from room to room and floor to floor, they found abundant evidence of a passion for collecting as intense as they had seen in Griffith's apartment and which Bogdanovic had noted in Wiggins's office. The walls displayed the memorabilia of Dodge's career as a journalist of the world and an author who had become a wealthy man by chronicling the lives and deeds of notorious criminals. Expensive furnishings proved he indulged an eclectic taste. Closets revealed a propensity for costly clothing. In the second-floor bedroom they discovered his homosexual nature in the form of oil paintings of nude young men and boys. On an antique bureau stood silver frames showcasing photographs of the same handsome, muscular, and sexually aroused youth. The largest of them had been inscribed: "To Jon with all my love, Jimmy C," in the large block lettering of a boyish hand.

"This is the part of being a cop that I've never gotten used to," Flynn said as she studied the smiling, almost cherubic face that made the rest of the photograph seem less obscene. "I hate poking around in a victim's private life, disturbing secrets."

Bogdanovic opened a large black-and-gold-laquered jewel box that looked Oriental in origin. "Somebody seems to have cleaned this out," he said. "And did you notice that things you'd expect to find in a house are also missing? I haven't seen one radio, TV set, stereo, or anything electronic and portable. My gut tells me that Jimmy Climax is the culprit."

Replacing the photograph, she said, "Are you proposing that this kid killed Dodge just to rip him off?"

"No, no. I think the kid found out that his lover wouldn't be coming home and helped himself to everything he thought he'd be able to convert to cash. More than likely, Jonathan Dodge's goods are already showing up for sale all over town. I suggest we invite Morgan Griffith down here as soon as possible. If he was Dodge's oldest and closest friend, he can probably give us a pretty good idea as to what's gone missing. If we're lucky we might be able to trace stuff that surfaces in the stolen goods market back to Jimmy Clements, a.k.a. Jimmy Climax. The kid might be able to give us a lead or two. Meantime, I'll order up a crime scene team to give this place a going over, so we'll know for sure if this is where the murder happened."

Led by a burly detective introduced to her as Al Leibholz, the faces that quickly appeared in the house were as new to Flynn as the surroundings. Yet all they did as they spread throughout the rooms in search of clues to a murder was as familiar to her as the work of the experts who had descended on Traitor's Lair. Soon after Bogdanovic's experts had appeared, Morgan Griffith arrived.

"We'll be very much in your debt if you'd let us impose on your time a little more," she said as they stood in the parlor. "We'd like you to sit down with Detective Leibholz and draw up a list of everything you notice as missing."

"It's not an imposition," he said, angrily. "I want that thieving little bastard caught and as many of Jonathan's things recovered as is possible. The idea of any of his possessions in the grubby hands of a fence or some sleazy pawnshop operator is enough to turn my stomach. Jonathan took care in drawing up his will to spell out what I, as the executor of his estate, was to do with his collections and his treasured personal souvenirs and memorabilia. As a matter of fact, I have an inventory of Jonathan's things. But I'm afraid it's already been transferred to Traitor's Lair along with other papers. I'll drive up tonight and dig it out. But I can tell you now that there's at least one item of value that kid didn't take. He left behind Jonathan's Maltese Falcon sword stick. He was too dumb to see the bird is silver."

"Excuse me," Flynn blurted. "Will you repeat that?"

"The Maltese Falcon is silver. And antique silver at that. It must be worth . . ."

"You said something about a sword."

Griffith nodded. "Yes. It's a sword stick. You give the top a twist, then draw the blade. This one is more like the swords used in fencing."

"A foil. Yes, that's what it could have been," Flynn said, grimly picturing Jonathan Dodge seated and unconscious or in a drunken stupor, his head tilted back, his mouth agape, and the long thin blade glinting in the light as it thrust forward. "It explains the puncture wound in Dodge's mouth. And the path in the brain that looked like it was made by an amazing disappearing bullet."

Bogdanovic knelt and studied the untouched walking stick. "Are you proposing this was the murder weapon?"

"I'm saying it's possible. Can you get Forensics to test it right away?"

"If this was how it was done, it's a first for me," he said. "And I'll wager my boss never came across anything like it in his mystery novels, either."

18

The Three-legged Game

WITH A YELLOW DUSK as background through the window behind his desk, the chief of detectives rocked slowly in a highback
leather chair and listened without interruption to a status report on
the murder of Jonathan Dodge. When Flynn and Bogdanovic finished, the rocking ceased and he placed his right arm upright on the
desk.

"Means. Motive. Opportunity," he said, raising a finger as he
spoke each word. "As we all learned in Police Academy, those are
the elements you need in the three-legged game of murder."

Lowering his hand, he inverted the fingers to form a tripod.

"You've found what appears to be the means. The sword."

The hand came down flat on the desk.

"What's the motive?"

Flynn shook her head. "We seem to have as many as the names
on the guest list at the Edgar Awards dinner."

"Who had the opportunity?" Goldstein said, tilting back in the
chair. "Out of that crowd at the dinner who took such delight in
imagining Dodge dead, someone crossed the line from thinking and
talking about it to actually go and do it. But why on that night? To
paraphrase the question we Jews ask one another at Passover,
'Why was Friday night different from every other night?' You two
are going to have to get the people on your list of motivated diners
to account for their time after the Edgars were handed out and then
sift out the one who's lying. As for this kid who was living with
Dodge, he might be able to help us with motive. Who can say what
Dodge may have confided to him during *après sex* pillow talk?
Johnny, I suggest you bring in Al Leibholz and Red Ryder to track

the kid down. Follow up on that theft angle, of course. But I think it is likely you'll find young Jimmy Climax trolling to pick up a new patron in gay bars catering to men of a certain age with the where-withal to become sugar daddies."

"Al is already on board," Bogdanovic said. "He's still at Gramercy Park wrapping up the crime scene and Red is—"

"Presumed crime scene," Flynn interjected.

With flushing cheeks, Bogdanovic repeated, *"Presumed* crime scene."

"What about Red?" Goldstein asked.

"He's on a two-week vacation."

"Not any more. Get hold of him wherever he is and tell him I said he's *off* vacation as of now. And make the arrangements for Arlene to have an office here in headquarters. We can't have her working out of a handbag. If you wish, Arlene, we can arrange a hotel room for you. That would save you commuting."

"I don't mind commuting. I get my best thinking done when I'm alone in my car."

"I'm sure you agree that the center of gravity in this case has shifted from Stone County to the city."

"I'll reserve judgment on that point, Chief," she said with a glance at Bogdanovic. "Until we know for sure where the murder was committed. As for the office, I accept your generous offer. About a hotel, I never sleep well in any bed but my own."

"Put a thriller in my mitt at bedtime," Goldstein said smiling, "and I can read myself to dreamland anywhere."

Flynn turned to Bogdanovic with a tenuous smile. "Johnny, what about you? Would I be wrong in assuming that, being an ex-Marine, you don't need to sleep at all?"

His reply was a steely stare.

"I think it's safe to assume nothing's going to develop on this case tonight," said the chief of detectives, "so let's call it a day, get a good night's rest in the bed of our choice, and return to the murder of Jonathan Dodge first thing tomorrow. Who do you propose to start with?"

"I'd like to know more about the party Wiggins threw after the dinner," Flynn said. "We know Dodge didn't attend. But I'm in the dark regarding who *was* there, when they arrived, and how long they stayed. I presume the one to ask is the person who hosted the affair."

"If you plan to begin with him, you can sleep in a little and avoid the morning rush-hour traffic into the city. The Usual Suspects opens at noon, and I've never heard of its proprietor rolling out of bed a moment before." Goldstein rose and extended a hand. "Then it's good night to you, Arlene, and please pass on my best regards to Aaron."

As she retrieved her bag from the floor next to her chair, Bogdanovic was brusque. "I'll walk you to your car."

"Thanks, but I know the way."

"To the elevator, then."

Shouldering the bag, she detected more than courtesy in his insistent tone. "If you wish."

Stepping into the corridor, he caught her sleeve and spoke sharply. "Look, I know you're feeling territorial about this case and you probably think that we're moving in fast to take it over. That's understandable. I'd feel the same if I were in your shoes. But you were way out of line in there, correcting me in front of my boss by saying, '*Presumed* crime scene.' You made me feel as if I were back in the Academy. It embarrassed the hell out of me."

"I'm sorry. It wasn't intentional. I know the rules of the game. If it turns out that Dodge was murdered here, I appreciate that it has to become your case. Don't be so goddamned sensitive. I'll meet you at noon and it's off to chat with Mr. Wiggins."

His frown faded and turned into a broad grin. "I'm sorry. I *was* being touchy. Let's meet at eleven. I'll treat you to a late breakfast. By the way, it's plain 'Wiggins.' There's no 'Mister.' No first name. And no one quite like him, either. You'll see for yourself."

19

Curious Incident in the Night

DIRECTLY UPON REACHING HOME, Flynn sat on the bed, kicked off her shoes, and phoned Benson. From the hubbub of children's voices in the background as he answered she judged that she had interrupted the Bensons at dinner. "If this is a bad time," she apologized, "I can call back in an hour when the kids are more settled."

He laughed. "Believe me, these four holy terrors don't get any more settled unless they're in bed. And even then I think they lie awake cooking up new plots to get me. Speaking of zoos, how's it going down there in Harvey Goldstein's menagerie?"

Crisply summarizing the day's events in the restrained manner to which he had become accustomed, Flynn could not suppress a surge of excitement as she told him of the discovery of the sword cane. "Of course we can't say for sure it's the murder weapon," she concluded, checking her emotions. "We have to wait for the lab report. But Johnny Bogdanovic ordered them to expedite it, so we'll know soon. We could find out as early as tomorrow. But thank God for Griffith. If we hadn't called him to Dodge's house to check on what was stolen, we might never have found out about that sword stick."

"Griffith ought to thank God himself. Telling you about that sword clears him of suspicion, doesn't it? I mean, I never met a murderer I didn't already have the goods on who obligingly came up to me and said, 'By the way, here's the weapon I did it with.' Maybe I should rethink Griffith's proposition to be an unofficial assistant on this case. He might prove helpful in other ways."

"He does bring us the plus of having known Dodge longer and

better than anyone. He's also got a personal stake in bringing Dodge's killer to book. If someone dumped a corpse on my door-step I'd be damned eager to help the police catch him, even if I weren't a writer smelling a book in it somewhere down the line."

"Do you really think Dodge's killer wanted to make Griffith out to be the killer?"

"I doubt very much if the person who killed Dodge truly be-lieved he could pin the deed on Griffith. This guy is smart. He would know that we would ask ourselves why Griffith would kill Dodge and then leave his body in a place Griffith knew was going to be visited that very weekend by a man hired to tear down the boathouse. I think the killer just wanted Griffith to sweat. He hoped to watch him twisting slowly in the wind. Why he wanted to see Griffith suffer is anybody's guess at this point, including Griffith's apparently."

"For that scenario to work the murderer has to have known Griffith was planning to have the boathouse demolished on that weekend."

"He may have. Griffith told everyone he knew that he had bought Traitor's Lair. He probably also told them of his plans to improve the place. Regardless of that, the body would have been discovered sooner or later, wouldn't it? Fulmer's arrival on the scene may just have been a coincidence, a happily serendipitous surprise. The killer didn't have to wait to savor the second part of his scheme. He wound up achieving the dual purpose of killing Dodge and putting Dodge's pal Griffith into the hot seat in one fell swoop. If the sword stick was the murder weapon and removes Griffith as a suspect, we've got to ask ourselves who would hate Griffith as much as he hated Dodge. Maybe more so. Because in my book it's a far worse fate to be sent to prison for life for a crime you didn't commit than to be murdered."

"The *real* motive for killing Dodge was to get at Griffith? A kind of revenge by proxy? I think you're onto something, Arlene. Fan-tastic—great work! What's next on your agenda?"

"Johnny Bogdanovic and I are questioning a man by the name of Wiggins. I gather he's some kind of world-of-mystery guru. He threw a party at his bookstore after the Edgar Awards dinner. But that's in the morning. My agenda right now calls for me to scrub off the grime and grit of a day in New York City by steaming in the shower for about an hour."

Drowned out by childish squeals, Benson had to shout: "You deserve it. Enjoy, enjoy!"

Tingling with pleasure in a cone of drumming water that felt as sharp as needles prickling her flesh, Flynn found herself imagining again the horrible manner in which Dodge had met his death and praying that he had not been aware of the atrocity, then wondering if prayer could work retroactively.

Might today's appeal to Almighty God already have been heard and answered? Had such a question been dealt with and gone by her unheard in the catechism classes of girlhood conducted by severe nuns and patient priests? They had taught her that because God existed throughout time, He knew all that had happened since the creation of the world, what was happening today, and what would be happening in the future. Could they also have covered retroactive prayer at a moment when her thoughts wandered, as they often had, rushing forward in time to imagine herself a woman?

But never, she remembered as the water beat the tiredness out of her, had she imagined herself carrying a police shield in her wallet and a .38 pistol in her handbag and investigating the greatest sin of all—premeditated murder.

Squeezing her eyes shut, she pictured the glint of light on the long, thin shaft of steel going into Jonathan Dodge's gaping mouth. Had death come instantly? Painlessly? If she prayed now that it be without pain, could she make it so? If she prayed very hard, could she even stop the murder? Had Dodge uttered a sound? Or had the terrible thing been done silently?

Suddenly aware of the pelting of the water on the shower curtain, she found herself remembering the terror of another murder committed with the thrust of a glinting steel blade. She had cowered in a movie theater, closing her eyes and covering her ears with her hands to shut out the agony of Janet Leigh being butchered in the shower in *Psycho*. When she opened her eyes, it was to see the blood mixed with water swirling down the drain. Years later she had been told that in the black and white movie the blood had been chocolate syrup. Although she had seen many murders in films made in color, not a drop of their blood had been as convincing.

In going through Jonathan Dodge's house in Gramercy Park, she did not expect to find blood. As Dr. Zeligman had pointed out, that was the genius of the way in which Dodge had been killed. His blood had remained within him, save for whatever amount may have clung to the murder weapon.

Realizing that she had not informed Zeligman of the discovery of the sword, she finished her shower and tried his number at the morgue but got the hospital switchboard. "The doctor has gone for the day," a woman said. "Do you have an emergency?"

"No. No emergency. Thank you." Hanging up, Flynn wondered what sort of an emergency required a coroner, then realized for the first time that Zeligman was also a physician and probably had a regular practice. A call to his home was taken by an answering machine, referring callers to the hospital number. Looking at the bedside clock, she calculated that thirty-six hours had passed since Benson phoned her about a possible homicide at Traitor's Lair. Assuming that the old man who had declared Jonathan Dodge a victim of murder was probably in bed, she decided to wait until morning to tell him the answer to the riddle of the amazing disappearing bullet.

Switching off the bedroom light, she welcomed the dark and the quiet, and felt glad that she did not live in a city. A moment later she drifted to sleep.

When the phone rang, she thought she had slept through the night. The clock said midnight, barely three hours after she had closed her eyes.

Benson's urgent voice said, "The state police barracks at Rocky Ridge just got off the horn with me. They got a frantic call from our friend Griffith at Traitor's Lair."

With a flash of irritation she groaned, "What's he want?"

"He says somebody just took a shot at him. The troopers are on the way, but I think you'd better go up there. It's a hell of an hour and I know you must be beat, but . . ."

"I'm halfway out the door."

"Call me as soon as you find out what the hell's going on."

Half an hour later the headlights of her car cutting across the parking area in front of Griffith's house caught him pacing frantically. Staring toward her, he stopped, looking like a startled deer caught in the middle of the road. As she approached, she saw a slight gash on the right side of his forehead and a trickle of dried blood around the corner of his eye.

"This is nothing," he said, gingerly touching the wound. "I got it seated at my desk in the library. I was going over the inventory of Jonathan's possessions when all of a sudden I heard something strike the window."

They strode to the house.

"I thought it was a bird that was drawn by the light. Then I found the window cracked around a hole. It was a bullet hole. I found where the slug went into the opposite wall. The damn thing must have missed hitting me by no more than an inch or two. One little shard of flying glass did get me. But it was so slight I didn't notice it until after I called for the police. I'm still waiting for the state cops to get here."

"Show me the bullet holes."

As they entered the house, she heard the wailing of a state police siren rapidly approaching.

Examining a splintered wood panel in the library, she found a flattened bullet. Turning, she asked, "Did you see or hear anything unusual before the shot?"

"There was a dog barking down by the river."

"What was strange about that?"

"I'd never heard one barking around here at night before."

20

Witness for the Prosecution

THE NEXT MORNING, Bogdanovic sipped and set down a mug of coffee. "That bullet certainly changes this case."

Flynn nibbled a corner of thin, crisp, dry toast. "Does it?"

Looking around the crowded coffee shop that hissed with whispers, she found serious men and women with attorneys' briefcases and others whose drawn, anxious expressions marked them as their clients in cases pending in the imposing city, state, and federal courthouses in and around Foley Square. Scattered among them sat pairs of cops in uniform. Two middle-aged men in suits struck her immediately as plainclothes detectives. Three younger men in jeans, sweatshirts, and sneakers, she decided, had to be a team of undercovers working narcotics. Still others bore the dazed and bored looks of citizens summoned to jury duty.

"Apparently it's open season on mystery writers," Bogdanovic continued, drawing her eyes back to him. "Whoever killed Dodge also shot at Griffith."

"Lots of hunters prowl those woods around Traitor's Lair."

"At night? I'm sorry."

"Griffith said he heard a dog barking."

Bogdanovic slurped coffee and again set down the cup. "Next thing, you'll be telling me it was the Hound of the Baskervilles."

"Hunters use dogs."

He shook his head violently. "It doesn't compute."

"What doesn't compute is why the person who killed Dodge up close and personal abruptly changed his modus operandi to make an attempt on Griffith's life long distance."

"In the Marines they teach you that in working out tactics you must take into account the situation and the terrain. Dodge presented one situation and terrain. Griffith another."

"I wasn't in the Marines."

He smiled. "You'd have been a hell of a drill instructor."

"Really?"

"You have just the right bitchiness."

"I might have joined, but back then they weren't interested in a few good women," she said, reaching for the check.

He snatched it away. "I said this was my treat."

"Only if it goes on your expense account."

"Very well. It's Goldstein's treat."

Fifteen minutes later, they stood before the Usual Suspects bookstore.

A sign in the window of a scarlet door said:

HOURS: NOON TO MIDNIGHT
IF CLOSED AND IF YOU MUST HAVE A BOOK
AT THIS MINUTE, KNOCK VERY LOUDLY

Below it hung another notice.

THANK YOU FOR NOT ASKING
THE PROPRIETOR AND PATRONS
TO REFRAIN FROM SMOKING

As they entered, a voice boomed from deep in the back of the store. "Sergeant B!"

Speeding toward them with surprising grace, Wiggins dodged book displays and two browsing customers, his enormous arms flung wide open.

Bogdanovic deftly sidestepped an embrace.

The arms fell heavily against bulging sides. "You naughty boy. You disappointed me, Sergeant. I expected you to come round yesterday to grill me about Jonathan's murder." Black eyes like marbles peered suspiciously at Flynn through fleshy slits. "Do I know this enchanting person?"

"This is Arlene Flynn, the chief investigator for District Attorney Aaron Benson of Stone County."

"Ah! Direct from the scene of the crime!"

"Why did you expect Sergeant Bogdanovic yesterday?"

"I was sure I'd be the prime suspect. Now here it is Tuesday and not so much as a plainclothesman lurking across the street in a doorway to keep an eye on me. If this gets out, it could be bad for business." He sighed. "Imagine Jonathan being found murdered in the wilderness. What on earth was a sophisticated New Yorker doing up there anyway?"

"Isn't Morgan Griffith a New York sophisticate?"

"A true sophisticate gets himself bumped off in his own tux. Griffith *rents.* Since it's obvious I'm not your *suspecto numero uno,* am I to be chief witness for the prosecution? Come with me into my lair and I'll tell *all* you need to know. If you'd come Monday, the case would be solved already."

"Solve it for us now," Flynn said, following him through the long, narrow aisles.

Wiggins turned abruptly. "Excuse me, Sergeant B, which of you is going to conduct this interrogation?"

Bogdanovic pointed. "Arlene is lead investigator."

Wiggins sighed. "Where was I?"

"You were saying that if we'd questioned you yesterday, the case should be solved by now," Flynn said.

"Exactly. It's open and shut," Wiggins said, pausing at a book rack to straighten an askew Mary Higgins Clark. "That kid did it. The one who was sponging off Jonathan. Jimmy Clements."

"How do you know? Did he confess?"

"A confession wasn't necessary. His actions proved louder than words. He was here Saturday morning as soon as the store opened, trying to sell me a first edition of *Murder in the Calais Coach.* That was the title Agatha Christie gave *Murder on the Orient Express* originally, in case you didn't know. Jonathan's first edition of *Calais* was signed by Dame Agatha. Not as Dame Agatha, just plain Agatha. She got Damed later. Naturally, I probed young Clements as to how and why he was peddling one of Jonathan's most prized possessions."

"What did Clements tell you?" Flynn asked.

As Wiggins opened the office door, Bogdanovic bent close to her and whispered, "Brace yourself, Arlene. This office is even more like a museum than Griffith's place."

"Please do not ask the question I hear from every woman who steps into this room," Wiggins admonished. "They all want to know who dusts. I've never had a man ask me that. The answer is, 'No one dusts.' To tidy up this office would be akin to mending the cannonball holes in the American flag that flew over Fort McHenry whilst Francis Scott Key wrote 'The Star-Spangled Banner.' Please take any seat you wish, Miss Flynn. There are no antiques. I am not like Jonathan in that respect. Due to my size, of course."

"It's a charming room, Wiggins," she said, choosing a cane bucket chair beneath a full-length, lifesize painting of Sherlock Holmes slouched in a similar one. The artist's signature, she noted, was Vernon Ney. "You were telling us about Jimmy Clements and the book."

"The liar said Jonathan gave it to him so that he could sell it to finance a trip to see his sick mother, as if I'd fall for such a blatant falsehood," Wiggins continued, closing the door. "Well, I didn't buy it. Nor the book. I phoned Jonathan's number immediately. I got no answer. When I turned around, the kid was gone. So was the Christie first edition. And so were several copies of the new P. D. James novel from a display rack by the front door. I am not what you'd call 'good in the sprint,' so the bastard made a clean getaway down Fifty-first Street to First Avenue and into the mists. I presume he rushed elsewhere to peddle his goods."

Bogdanovic leaned against the door. "How do you turn this episode with Clements into his murdering Jonathan?"

"Believe me, Sergeant B, to get that book out of Jonathan's abode, you would have to kill him. It was not only that Jonathan collected rare editions of mystery titles. He was a train buff. He owns a loft down in TriBeCa that has not a thing in it but an enormous model railroad layout. It's quite common for people who love mysteries to be railway fans, though the phenomenon is most prevalent in the male animal. Jonathan was considering buying his own private railway carriage—one of those romantic cars with the open observation platform at the end that men who ran for President used to make speeches from on whistle-stopping campaigns. I ribbed Jonathan about it, asking him if he were planning to seek the highest office in the land himself. Jonathan was not amused. I assume he felt himself more than qualified to do so."

"Getting back to Jimmy Clements," Flynn said. "If the kid murdered Jonathan for financial gain, as you imply, wouldn't the body have been found in the Gramercy Park house? How would Clements get it all the way to Stone County and into Griffith's boathouse? And why?"

"Really, Miss Flynn," he replied with a dismissive wave of a pudgy hand, "I can't provide you all the niggling details."

"If we can put Clements out of the picture for a moment," said Bogdanovic, "I'd like to fathom your recollection of the reception you held here in the store after the Edgar Awards."

"You attended. You probably remember it better than I."

"I'm not the chief witness for the prosecution."

"What do you want to know?"

"Who else was here?"

"Chief Goldstein, of course. But I presume you have eliminated him from your suspect list."

"He's got an alibi," Flynn said, glancing at Bogdanovic.

"Typical of cops. Raise a question about one and the whole force rallies to erect the 'blue wall of silence' around him."

"Look, fellas," Flynn said impatiently, "can we please cut out the snappy repartee and stick to business?"

Wiggins rolled his eyes at Bogdanovic. "Oh my, Sergeant B, she is *strict*. She takes all the fun right out of murder."

"I find nothing amusing in a sword shoved in a man's brain."

Wiggins's ruddy face went pale. "God, is that what it was?"

"The murder weapon appears to have been Dodge's own sword stick," Bogdanovic answered.

"The prized Maltese Falcon?"

"That information hasn't been made public, so please keep it to yourself. Okay?"

"You have my oath, Sergeant B. What a ghastly way to die. I find it hard to believe that anyone I know would be capable of such a thing. They're all so entertaining. On the other hand, Eva Braun thought Hitler was a lot of laughs, didn't she? But why do you assume Jonathan's murderer attended my post-Edgars fête?"

"We have to start somewhere."

"Most of the guests were from our table at the dinner."

"The very ones who'd amused themselves discussing ways to murder Dodge."

"I also invited a few MWA officers who were at Table One. And all of the award recipients came."

"Except Dodge. You were angry at him for stiffing you."

"Of course I was. I took it as an affront, not only to yours truly but to the organization that had just bestowed its highest honor on him. Now it appears that he was prevented from attending because he was either already dead or about to be. I see why you're interested in who was here."

"Not only who was here," Flynn said, "but anyone who came late or left earlier than you might have expected."

"I follow the way you're thinking," Wiggins said excitedly. "You believe it's possible that the murderer did the dastardly deed, left the body wherever the act took place, and came to the party to establish an alibi. He disposed of it after the party."

Bogdanovic nodded. "That's one scenario."

"Let me see. Who came late? Vernon Ney was tardy; he didn't stay long, either. There were the ladies, Elvira Eveland and Maggie Tinney. They arrived a few minutes after you and Chief Goldstein, as I recall. They came in with Alex Somerfield, and all three stayed to the very end. I put the ladies in a cab."

"Did Somerfield go with them?"

"Alex decided to walk. He's into keeping fit, you see."

"From Beekman Place to the Seventy-ninth Street Marina is quite a hike."

"Alex could have managed it with Elvira under one arm and Maggie the other. Or with me sitting on his shoulders."

"The artist who's painting your portrait looked like he was in rather good physical shape, as well."

"I have no doubt Vern Ney is capable of handling himself. I see what you're getting at! Lugging Jonathan's dead body would require more than a modicum of strength. That means you can cross puny Myron Frank off the list of likelies, Sergeant."

"He could have had help," Flynn said.

"Wait a minute! Myron came directly here with me. Soon after us, Morgan Griffith arrived. Since Myron was with me the entire time, he could not have killed Jonathan before the party."

"When did he leave?"

After a moment of thought, Wiggins lifted his massive shoulders in a shrug. "Sorry. I didn't notice."

"He didn't say thanks and good night to the host?"

"Social amenities have never been Myron's strong suit. That may be why he's such a killer agent. Oops! No insinuation there!"

"How much resentment did Frank harbor over Dodge dropping him as his agent?"

"I know his feelings were hurt. But Myron's cut of Jonathan Dodge books would have feathered the Frank nest for the rest of Myron's life. The same is true for Oscar Pendleton. His publishing firm's back list of Dodge titles is a gold mine."

"There was one guest listed for Table Two who didn't put in an appearance at the dinner. . . ."

"You refer to Jack Bohannon."

"Did he come to the party?"

"The rascal did not."

"Has he been in touch with you to explain why he missed the dinner and the reception?"

After ruminating a moment, Wiggins smiled slyly. "From what I know of Jack Bohannon, Sergeant B, if he were planning to kill Jonathan, he would have worked out an alibi. Or at least the illusion of one. Jack's entire life has been smoke and mirrors. If you wish me to, I'll phone him now and ask where he was on Friday night. However, Oscar Pendleton may have discerned the reason that evening. You'll recall that Oscar got to the dinner late on account of the storm and suggested Bohannon could have become stranded on the highway. I'd bet that's exactly what happened."

"Thanks for the offer to call Bohannon," Flynn said. "But we'd prefer to chat with him ourselves. Incidentally, I understand his magic act includes a trick with a sword."

"Yes, I've seen him perform it often. He creates a spectacular illusion in which he appears to accidentally run a beautiful girl through with a fencing foil."

21

A Linking Clue

SQUINTING in the bright sun, a sinewy youth with blond hair and white shorts that accented a sun-bronzed bare torso jerked his thumb toward the river. "Mr. Somerfield went out on *Karla* early Saturday morning."

"Do you have any idea when he'll be back?" Bogdanovic asked.

"He didn't say."

"How about his destination?"

"I wouldn't know about that. There's no reason for me to, is there?"

"I thought perhaps a marina would maintain a record of arrivals and destinations of departures like they do at airports."

"The people who keep their boats here come and go as they please. Unless they've got an oceangoing craft and are coming in from a foreign port. Then the Coast Guard and Customs require us to keep records. They think everyone who owns a boat that goes to sea is dealing drugs."

Flynn looked away from him at dozens of sailboats and motorized craft of all sizes. Moored to the right and left on the east shore of the Hudson, they were the sad remnants of a waterfront that once felt the kiss of prows of magnificent oceanliners with regal names—the queens of the Atlantic, *Elizabeth* and *Mary,* and the *Empress of Britain*—as romantic as their distant ports of call—*Normandie, Bremen, Caledonia, Rotterdam.* Now the river and the harbor to which it flowed seemed as anachronistic as the old radio in Morgan Griffith's cluttered library in the ghostly house at Traitor's Lair.

"If a normal pleasure craft were going for a cruise around the harbor or up the river," she said, "you'd have no record?"

The youth hooked his thumbs on the loops of his beltless shorts and leaned against a rail, his back to the boats. "That's right."

"How about at night?" Bogdanovic asked.

"The only record we'd have is if the boat got fueled up."

"I understand Mr. Somerfield lives on his boat."

"Except in winter. Then he takes *Karla* down to Key West. But come May first he's back. Stays till the end of September, usually."

"May I leave my business card with you? Should you see him, please pass on that I'd appreciate a call."

He looked warily at the card without taking it. "Is there gonna be some kind of trouble?"

Bogdanovic pressed the card into the youth's palm. "If there were, I wouldn't be leaving this, would I?"

With a shrug, the youth tucked it into a pocket.

Turning to Flynn, Bogdanovic sighed. "New York in summer and the Caribbean in winter. How's that for the sweet life?"

"I prefer the mountains."

"These boats have given me a hankering for seafood," he said as they strode to their car. "How about lunch? They say that fish is brain food. Maybe all we need to crack this case is a thick slab of grilled salmon. Or are you a meat-and-potatoes person?"

"A light seafood salad will do nicely," she said, getting into the car. "As long as it's a quick lunch."

"We'll zip down to South Street Seaport. And after we eat, we can drop in at headquarters and see if the lab report on the sword stick has come in. I've told Detective Leibholz to keep the pressure on. And if we're lucky, Red Ryder will be back. If anyone's going to track down Jimmy Clements, it'll be Al and Red. I think that kid showing up at the Usual Suspects Saturday morning proves what I said when we were going through Dodge's house, that he knew Dodge was dead, probably killed him, and helped himself to everything he could carry away and cash in. I'll bet you that empty box I found in Dodge's bedroom was crammed with expensive jewelry. Having seen Dodge's taste in clothes, I'd say that box contained watches, rings, cuff links. You name it."

"Of course," she exclaimed. *"Cuff links.* Very good, Johnny. Very, very good. I believe you may have crossed Jimmy Clements's name off our suspect list."

"How the hell do you figure that?"

"If the kid murdered Dodge to steal his valuables, how come he didn't take the diamond cuff links Dodge was wearing? And why not the matching tuxedo shirt studs? And the Rolex watch? And a wallet full of money and credit cards? Instead, he shows up at Wiggins's door on Saturday morning with a book that could bring him a couple of hundred dollars at the most. Why that Saturday?"

Bogdanovic thought for a moment, then blurted, "Because he knew Dodge was dead."

"At the start of this case, when Griffith mentioned that Dodge had a boy for his lover," she said, "I thought the kid would be a bit player, at most, in this drama. Suddenly, he has moved centerstage. We've got to go all out to find him, Johnny. He may be our star witness. He's got to be the highest priority for Leibholz and . . . what's his partner's name?"

"Reiter. R-E-I-T-E-R. His name's Joe but everybody calls him 'Red' because of his hair and 'Ryder,' as in R-Y-D-E-R. Like the character in the old cowboy movies. His sartorial hallmark is a pair of snakeskin western boots. Red should be coming back from his aborted vacation later today."

"Can you set up a meeting for tomorrow morning early with him and Leibholz? Assuming Chief Goldstein will want to sit in, maybe we can hold it in his office. How's ten o'clock?"

Promptly at that hour, Goldstein introduced Reiter. As tall and rangy as his nickname suggested, he settled onto a couch at Leibholz's side and for the next half-hour listened to Flynn's summation of facts, suppositions, suspects, questions that had been answered and those that had not. Speaking without notes, she sounded at times like a lecturer at the Police Academy, but mostly she held them spellbound with a tale of a real murder that came across as though she had read it in a novel.

At last, standing at a large window affording a breathtaking panoramic view of the northerly sprawl of Manhattan, she came to the disappearance of Jimmy Clements. Turning to face the men, she asked, "Do you think he's still in town? Or should we assume he's skipped by now?"

"It's been my experience," Leibholz replied, "and I'm sure Red will agree with me, that guys like Clements stick close to home, even if they do happen to be hot."

Reiter nodded assent. "It's a case of preferring the devil you know."

"Since he's suspected in the theft of Dodge's property," Bogdanovic interjected, "you've got sufficient cause to pick him up and hold him without paperwork. I don't want any time wasted waiting for a warrant."

"We're fortunate in that we have an inventory of the stuff he took from Dodge's house," Flynn added.

"The list will be circulated to the pawnshops and second-hand stores," Goldstein said, "as well as throughout the diamond district in Midtown and the jewelers along Canal Street."

"Is the word out that Clements is wanted?" asked Reiter.

"Though there's been nothing in the press about him," Flynn said, "I think you have to assume that he's not stupid and that he figures the police will be looking for him."

"As I said to Miss Flynn," Goldstein continued, "I think he is probably going to turn up in the bars patronized by older gay men in hopes of finding someone to take Dodge's place. So you'll know who you're looking for; the photo lab has supplied copies of a picture found in Dodge's bedroom."

"Raunchy parts cropped," Bogdanovic said with a leer.

"While you guys hunt for Clements," Flynn said, "Johnny and I will be dashing round town chatting with what I think I'm right in calling the most curious collection of characters anyone in this room has ever encountered in a single case. But the moment you've got Clements in custody, give us a shout, no matter what the time of day or night."

PART FIVE

An Exact Science

Detection is, or ought to be, an exact science, and should be treated in the same cold and unemotional manner.

—SHERLOCK HOLMES IN *THE SIGN OF FOUR*

Detection requires a patient persistence which amounts to obstinacy.

—CHIEF SUPERINTENDENT ADAM DALGLEISH IN P. D. JAMES'S *AN UNSUITABLE JOB FOR A WOMAN*

22

Point of Interest

CROSSING THE SURPRISINGLY spacious living room of a small Cape Cod–style house on a tree-shaded street of similarly neat homes behind well-groomed lawns in the heart of Kew Gardens, Arlene Flynn experienced an eerie sensation of being followed by the eyes of a lifesize bronze bust in the middle of the fireplace mantel. A brass plate at the base bore one name:

HOUDINI

Examining the statue, she addressed its owner, a tall, lean man of middle years with a gray-streaked brown Van Dyke beard. "I trust it's a good likeness, Mr. Bohannon."

"The sculptor did it from life. However, I've never had the privilege of meeting Houdini. Perhaps I'll realize that dream one of these years by seeing him materialize at our annual séance."

"I dimly recall reading an article about that event. Houdini fans get together on Hallowe'en and try to summon his spirit. He promised that if he found there was another side, he'd communicate from there. Is that correct?"

"I've had the honor of presiding at the gatherings over the past several years. Alas, the voice of Houdini has yet to reach us from that distant shore."

"Very few people become so famous that their name defines them," she said. "Jesus, of course. Napoleon. Churchill. Ike. Hitler. Stalin. Garbo. Gable. *Houdini.* Because you are such an authority on him, and having seen how some of your friends in the Mystery Writers of America turned rooms into museums for their idols, I expected to find your home brimming with Harry Houdini artifacts."

"I share this house with my wife and three kids. My museum is confined by mutual agreement to the basement. This bust is the only exception. Everything connected to my magic act is also down there. But you haven't come all the way to Queens to talk about Houdini or watch me do tricks, have you? You want to ask me about Friday night."

Bogdanovic smiled. "Do you also read minds?"

"Wiggins called me to expect somebody to ask why I was a no-show at the Edgars dinner and at Wiggy's reception. I assumed I'd get a phone call. The explanation for my absence is quite simple. There was a ferocious rainstorm Friday night. Foolishly, I tried to plow through a huge pool beneath an overpass. My car's engine flooded out. Fortunately, a couple of guys that were in back of me got out of their cars and helped push me out, or I might have drowned."

"Did you know them?"

"They were just a couple of good Samaritans. They got back in their cars and drove off. The opposite way, of course."

"Did you call a towing service?"

"I just left that heap there, walked home and went back for it in the morning. I was sort of hoping somebody might have stolen it. I would have used the insurance settlement to make a down payment on a new chariot. What amazed me was that the old crate started, in spite of the drenching it got. Up to the roof."

Flynn asked, "Was anyone with you Friday night? Your wife?"

"Barbara teaches Friday nights. I was by myself."

"When did your wife return home?"

"She knew I'd be out till the wee hours, so she made arrangements to spend Friday night at her mother's house."

"Were your children here?"

"They're married or away in college."

"So you were home alone."

He lifted his arms as if to produce a trick. "I guess that leaves me with no alibi."

"What did you do when you got home?"

"I went straight down to the basement to tinker with a new

illusion I've been developing. However, it does not involve using a sword. And I assure you that the sword I do employ in the act could not have killed Jonathan. The blade telescopes. There is no way I could have used it to murder anyone. I'll show you. Come to the basement."

They followed him down a steep stairway to a large, brightly lit room and entered what appeared to be a carnival sideshow. The walls were almost covered by posters of Houdini and the names and images of other magicians. Gaudily painted trunks, boxes, and crates stood everywhere.

Examining a red and yellow guillotine, Flynn asked, "Why do you think Dodge was killed with a sword?"

Bohannon opened an ancient steamer trunk emblazoned with: THE AMAZING BOHANNON'S WONDERFUL WORLD OF WIZARDRY AND ILLUSION. "Don't tell me that Wiggins made that story up."

"How did you feel when you heard that Dodge was murdered, Mr. Bohannon?"

"Unsurprised," he said, removing a long fencing foil from the trunk and slashing the air. Holding it at arm's length with both hands, he directed the point to his chest, then thrust it downward until the hilt pressed flat against his shirt. "See? It telescopes."

"Why were you unsurprised?" Flynn asked.

Bohannon passed her the sword. "The guy was a rat."

"Are you speaking on the basis of observation?" She handed the sword on to Bogdanovic. "Or is that hearsay?"

"Both. Personally, I found Jonathan Dodge a first-class bullshitter. Excuse the language. Long on talk, short on followthrough."

Bogdanovic returned the sword.

"He said he was going to put me in touch with a TV producer about developing an idea for a mystery show," Bohannon continued as the sword went back into the trunk. "It was to have a magician as the detective. Well, I wound up spending months writing sample scripts. But when I called him up a couple of days before the MWA dinner, he told me he would be going out of the country to research a book he was working on and that when he got back he'd be too busy for what he called—and I quote him exactly—'a lame-brained television show that has a snowball's chance in hell of being produced.' I was furious. I *felt* like killing him. But I didn't.

How could I? My car was out of commission."

Bogdanovic shrugged. "So you say."

"Ask the guys who gave me the push!"

"Ah! That would be a neat trick, sir. Considering that you can't give us their names and there is no alibi witness in your hat or up your sleeve to vouch for your story."

"Wait a minute! I think I do have an alibi witness. What about my car?"

"What about it?"

"The underpass filled up with water. It rose right up to the roof of the car. The inside really got soaked. The seats still haven't dried out. It's parked in the driveway. Take a look."

"We'll check it out, Mr. Bohannon," Flynn said. "Thanks for your time. Good luck with your new illusion. And the TV show. I hope I'll see it on the air soon. I'm a big fan of mysteries. No need to show us the way out."

"The car's unlocked," he shouted as they climbed the steps. "You'll see how wet it is inside."

Pressing down on the upholstery of the front and back seats of the four-door sedan, Bogdanovic muttered, "There's no doubt in my mind that this car was submerged. These seats didn't get this wet on account of the windows being down in the rain."

Flynn nodded. "They're as soggy as the earth was around the boathouse at Traitor's Lair on Sunday."

"If it rained as hard up there as it did in the city over the weekend, whoever killed Dodge must have gotten soaked to the skin toting that body."

Flynn closed the door of Bohannon's car and leaned against it. Thinking hard, she grimaced. "But Dodge's tuxedo *wasn't.*"

"The tuxedo wasn't what?"

"Soaked! As I recall, it wasn't even damp."

"Okay, the rain was somehow kept off the body. Wet or dry, what's it matter?"

"It's just one of those interesting little questions which seem to pop up in every investigation that make a case incomplete until they're answered."

"Meanwhile, who's next on our interview list?"

"First, the rejected artist. Then the jilted publisher."

23

Portrait of a Cad

FROM FLOOR TO CEILING and running the breadth of the top-floor loft, a slanted window flooded northern light into a long, narrow room. Suffused with the rich smell of wet oil pigments, the studio was bordered by rows of untouched canvases that leaned against walls adorned with framed portraits of men, women, and children, Spanish landscapes, and several paintings of matadors in radiant suits of light. Another caught the color and excitement of the running of the bulls in Pamplona. Two depicting bullfights flanked a stuffed and mounted head of an earless bull. Below was a plaque displaying a pair of crossed bullfight swords.

At the center of the studio, surrounded by a huge canvas dropcloth, a large wooden easel supported an unfinished lifesize painting of Wiggins draped in his lavish Oriental robe. Holding a thickly laden palette in his left hand and a foot-long brush in his right, a husky young man with a trim brown beard and a paint-smeared gray smock daubed the fleshy face with featherlike strokes of pink.

"The idea that I'd kill someone because he didn't like my portrait of him and refused to pay for it is ludicrous," he said furiously. "I'd turn the matter over to my lawyer and sue him."

"In this case, Mr. Ney," Flynn said, "the subject sued *you.*"

"For slander! What a charade. Jonathan was indulging in his favorite sport of making someone's life miserable. My time had come to be the son of a bitch's flavor of the month."

"If you knew he was such a son of a bitch, why did you agree to take his money to paint his portrait?" Bogdanovic demanded.

Ney abandoned the palette and turned to face him. "I like money as much as anyone, Sergeant. But money was not the reason I agreed to paint him."

115

"What was the reason?"

"It may sound silly."

Bogdanovic gazed up at the earless bull. "Try us."

"I needed someone like Jonathan for my portfolio. I have a color photograph taken of each portrait I paint and the best go into a book that I show to prospective clients. Until I painted Jonathan, the portfolio lacked someone of his maturity. I wanted someone distinguished, with gray hair. He also had great jowls."

"May we see the picture?" Flynn asked.

"Jonathan not only refused to pay. He never gave it back. I assume it's stored somewhere in his house. Maybe his lawyer has it. I don't know where it is. The worst part of this affair is that I didn't have a chance to get it photographed. Now that he's dead, I guess I'll have to ask my lawyer to get it from whoever is the executor of Jonathan's estate. I'm not sure it's worth going to all that trouble just for some gray hair and great jowls."

Flynn's eyes scanned the studio. "Bull fighting appears to be a dominant theme of your work when you're not doing portraits."

"If you take a close look at the running of the bulls, you'll find me to the right of the center bull."

She moved to the painting. "You appear to have had a close call. Did you? Or is this the artist's imagination?"

He laughed. "The beast almost gored me good. That was a few years ago when I was pretty agile and had an idea I might make a pretty good matador."

"Did you ever get into the ring?"

"Twice. First to find out if I had the guts. The second time to see if I had the right stuff. Both bulls survived me, although not the day. My romantic dream of achieving glory in the blood and sand of the arena also perished that afternoon. I still have my suit of lights. It's a little tight in the thighs and worse around the midsection."

Gingerly touching one of the crossed swords, she asked. "What do you call this?"

"It's an *estoque*. The matador uses it for the kill."

"They appear to be slightly bent near the end."

"The downward curve assures they strike the aorta."

Nodding, she lifted one of the swords from the plaque and

turned it upside down. "An interesting and ingenious device," she said, replacing it. "If I were to ask you to put on your mystery author's hat, what would your detective be doing at this point to solve the murder of Jonathan Dodge?"

He grinned. "He'd be questioning me. But this is not a case my fictional sleuth would handle. He's a detective who collects art and whose clients are always drawn from the world of art. I never saw Jonathan in an art museum. On the other hand, it's a puzzle that my sleuth would find challenging. So many characters, so many motives. And so thoroughly deserving a victim. As for me, my detective would go away persuaded I could not have done it."

"Why would that be? You have a double motive: money and your reputation."

"You attended the Mystery Writers dinner," said Bogdanovic. "Dodge died shortly afterward. Unless you're able to account for your time after the dinner, you had the opportunity."

"I went to a reception at the Usual Suspects bookstore. The owner, Wiggins, can vouch for that. You, too."

"You arrived late."

"It was raining. I couldn't get a cab. I walked."

"You also left early."

"I had to go to bed. I had work to do the next day."

Flynn asked, "Do you own a car, Mr. Ney? Perhaps a van?"

"I live in Manhattan. A car is a pain in the ass."

"What do you do if you have to leave the city?"

"I rent a car."

"Did you rent one last weekend?"

"If I had I wouldn't have gotten drenched on Seventh Avenue trying to hail a taxi, would I? Say! There's my alibi. Check with the cab driver who picked me up and took me to Wiggins' party."

"That's an easy task in novels, Mr. Ney," Bogdanovic said. "In real detective work it isn't that simple."

"I thought cab drivers had to keep trip sheets."

"Correct. And some do. Some don't. And some don't bother to turn on the meter. Did you ask your cabbie for a receipt?"

"Of course not. Why would I ask for a receipt? Would you?"

"No. But I'm not in need of someone or something to substantiate an alibi, am I?"

"By the way, how am I supposed to have killed him?"

"You could've used an *estoque*. Turned upside down, it would curve up into the brain," Flynn said.

Ney blanched. "Jonathan was stabbed in the head?"

"Through his mouth with a long thin blade, like a sword."

"Look, if you think I stuck Jonathan with an *estoque,* then take them with you. Send them to your crime lab. Test them for blood stains."

"There's no need to do that, Mr. Ney. Judging by the dust on these, they haven't been touched since you hung them. Of course, you could have had another *estoque.*"

"Search the studio. It's also where I live, so if I killed Jonathan, it was here. Take all the time you need. You'll find no other *estoque* around here."

"If a writer of your reputation were to hold on to a weapon he'd used for murder, I'd be surprised. And terribly disappointed. I'm sorry to have interrupted your work on the Wiggins portrait. I think he'll be delighted. It's a splendid likeness. By the way, Dodge's executor is Morgan Griffith."

24

Mysterious Doings

"COME IN, SERGEANT," said Oscar Pendleton from the doorway of his office that afternoon. "If you've come in connection with the murder of Jonathan Dodge, you're in luck. I'm wrapping up a meeting with Myron Frank. I assume you will want to talk to him as well. I'm delighted it's you handling the investigation."

Bogdanovic turned slightly toward Flynn. "Actually, the case is being handled by the Stone County D.A.'s staff. This is his chief investigator, Arlene Flynn. I'm her local liaison. Whether we talk to you together or one at a time is Arlene's call."

Pendleton stroked his silver beard. "Shall it be two against two, Miss Flynn, or would you prefer to gang up on us one at a time in hopes of catching inconsistencies in the story we've cooked up to cover our conspiracy? Is it to be good cop–bad cop?"

"If the two of you are conspirators," she said, interpreting jocular intent, "I credit the founder of Mysterious Doings, both store and publishing house, with being too savvy to have come up with a scenario filled with pitfalls. I think we can save us all time by making it two on two. Besides, I'm not an adherent of the view that nothing happens unless there is a conspiracy. I believe Lee Harvey Oswald was the lone assassin of President Kennedy, that Sirhan B. Sirhan killed Bobby Kennedy by himself, James Earl Ray shot Dr. Martin Luther King, Jr., on his own, Marilyn Monroe overdosed on drugs, and that nobody in the United States government hid the bodies of little green men from space in a hangar out in Arizona or New Mexico or wherever they're supposed to have come down from the skies in their flying saucer, unless and until someone shows me evidence otherwise."

"Shall I take it from that," Pendleton said, admitting them to his office, "that you are not looking for a conspiracy in Jonathan's murder?"

"You may take it that should I develop evidence of a conspiracy, everyone in it will be prosecuted vigorously by my boss, District Attorney Aaron Benson."

Two floors above the bookstore in a former town house, the office was at the rear in a cramped room piled high with books and manuscripts. Directing her and Bogdanovic to chairs with table arms like those in old schoolrooms, Pendleton said, "May I introduce Myron Frank?"

Extending a hand as Frank rose to greet her, she said, "I don't expect to keep you long, sir. I'm Arlene Flynn. You know Sergeant Bogdanovic."

Frank nodded and resumed his chair. "Indeed I do. The sergeant was a fascinating dinner companion."

"John informed me that you gentlemen shared a bond in your associations with Dodge. He walked out on you."

"That's right," Pendleton replied. "In my case it was for bigger money in the form of advances against royalties. But that is not a motive for murder. A lawsuit, maybe. Moot, now."

"Jonathan left me with the intention of self-representation," Frank said. "He had every right to. Our representation agreement was up for renewal."

"In not renewing he saved a fifteen percent commission on all his earnings?"

"Correct. I tried to get him to see that an author who acts as his own agent is as stupid as a lawyer defending himself in a trial. He has a fool for a client."

"Did he offer an explanation as to the timing of his break with either of you?"

"It was my experience as his agent that Jonathan was never interested in confiding his motives or taking advice gracefully."

"Am I right in believing that losing him as a client and as an author constitutes a severe economic blow?"

"Naturally, we'd prefer to have him," Frank said. "But he's still bound to us by the contracts for his past work."

"That is not an insignificant fact," interjected Pendleton.

"Please tell Sergeant Bogdanovic and me what you did after the MWA dinner."

"There was a reception at the Usual Suspects," Pendleton answered. "An Edgars Awards night is incomplete without a brandy and a cigar while Wiggins holds court. I came directly here after it. That was around one in the morning."

"Your store was open at that hour?"

"Mysterious Doings *Bookstore* closes at the witching hour. Mysterious Doings *Books* operates at all hours, especially when deadlines loom. I've got two titles that are a tad behind where they ought to be schedulewise. I worked on them for a couple of hours. All by my lonesome."

"I went straight home," said Frank.

"Are you married, Mr. Frank?"

"My wife was asleep. I was careful not to wake her up."

"Most considerate of you. Was there a reason for her not attending the dinner?"

"She finds them short on glamour. She edits romance novels."

"Are you married, Mr. Pendleton?"

"Cynthia has been in London for three weeks to pitch next spring's catalogue to the Brits. She's due home the day after tomorrow. She thought it important for the company to attend the memorial service for Jonathan that's being arranged by Jonathan's literary executor, Morgan Griffith."

Bogdanovic stirred and leaned forward, gripping the corner of the table chair. "What does 'literary executor' mean?"

"Griffith assumes control of that part of Jonathan's estate involving all his books, regarding copyrights, contracts, royalties, film deals—the works," Frank replied. "And then carries out whatever the last will and testament decreed."

"That must be an enormous responsibility."

"Indeed so. Poor Griffith."

Flynn frowned. "Why do you say 'poor Griffith'?"

"The poor guy was Jonathan's only friend, so he wound up stuck with a really thankless task. Unless one is a lawyer, why would anyone agree to be someone's executor? In Griffith's case it certainly wasn't in expectation of a big legacy. I happen to know that Jonathan's estate has been bequeathed to the University of

Iowa. Jonathan studied journalism there. So did Griffith, but a few years later. Jonathan made no secret of the fact that not one smidgen of his estate was going directly to any human being. He said to me once, in Griffith's presence, that to do so would be casting pearls before swine. Yet Griffith remained his friend."

"He told me he liked him. Admired him. Envied him."

"Granting that Dodge was an overall louse," Bogdanovic said, "has either of you any notion of what might have prompted the scene he had at the dinner with Elvira Eveland?"

Pendleton sighed. "Now you are asking us to decipher the mysteries of the Sphinx, for Elvira is just as inscrutable."

Frank wheezed a laugh. "And just about as old."

25

Sisters in Suspense

FROM ELVIRA EVELAND'S fifth-floor windows in the offices of Madison Square Books, the narrow facade of the triangular Flatiron Building two blocks south resembled the prow of an old gray ship bearing down on the green sea of treetops of the park from which the publishing firm took its name. She peered over manuscripts piled so high on her desk Flynn and Bogdanovic could barely see her. "When you telephoned to arrange an interview and explained its purpose, Miss Flynn," she said, "I took the liberty of asking my dearest friend and sister suspect to join the Third Degree."

Margaret Tinney perched like a bird at the edge of a chair adjacent to the desk and chirped, "It's so thrilling to be considered a murder suspect."

Bogdanovic gave her hand a tender pat. "Let's not use the word 'suspect.' Let's say 'witness.' "

"You should know at the outset that Maggie and I have no secrets," Eveland declared. "Of course, whether you two wish to question us together or separately is up to you."

"We're doing duets today." Bogdanovic chuckled.

Puzzled, Eveland lifted her head a little higher. "Would either of you care for coffee? A cup of tea, perhaps?"

"No, thank you," Flynn replied. "I'm a one-cup-a-day person."

Pressing down on the pile of paper, Eveland smiled across it at Bogdanovic. "What about you, handsome?"

"My caffeine intake is already at heart-attack level, Elvira."

"A wise decision on both your parts. Either brew would be of the instant-poison variety. Who's to get grilled first? Shall it be

Maggie or myself? There's nothing either of us could tell you that the other doesn't know, so you need not be concerned about asking embarrassing questions. And everyone knows neither of us held Jonathan in personal esteem, so there will be no revelations on that score. We did admire the *author* Jonathan Dodge greatly."

Tinney nodded. "He wrote superbly. Elvira hardly had to touch his manuscripts, even the first one Jonathan brought to her. That was the Boston Strangler murders."

"That's true. He was a pleasure to edit. We used to dispose of all my questions and suggestions for changes over a nice lunch at the Algonquin. I'm sure Oscar Pendleton found his craftsmanship just as outstanding after Jonathan left me to go with Oscar's fledgling publishing venture."

"When was that?"

"I don't recall the year. The book dealt with a murder in Vietnam at the height of that awful war. My mistake was Oscar Pendleton's gain. The book put his Mysterious Doings publishing house on the literary map."

"Why didn't you publish it?"

"Jonathan did not reveal the identity of the killer. He saw the story as one policeman's obstinacy in the face of all odds against him. When I told him I could not publish a book unless the bad guy got caught, he stormed out of this office and went straight uptown to Mysterious Doings. Understandably, dear Oscar recognized the pulling power of the name Jonathan Dodge on a book jacket, no matter what was inside. The rest is what they call publishing history. But it *was* an unsatisfactory book."

"At the dinner Friday night," Bogdanovic said, "Dodge made you very upset."

Eveland's eyebrows arched. "Did he?"

"He demanded to talk to you and all but dragged you from the dining room!"

"Oh, that was about a book I'm publishing. It's a marvelous read by Alexander Somerfield. So marvelous that we're keeping it under wraps until publication date. Somehow Jonathan got wind of it. Jonathan has always been jealous of Alex. He demanded to see the manuscript. I told him that would be improper and irregular. I kept putting him off, dodging him. No pun intended. I didn't take or return his calls. When I saw him at the Edgars, I almost didn't go into the dining room. The skunk sandbagged me. He kidnapped me to the men's room. The *men's* room! I got him off my back by promising that if he came around to my office Saturday morning before he departed town on his voyage, I would give him a peek at the manuscript. That was a fib. I knew he would be leaving the country Saturday afternoon and I had no intention of meeting him in the morning. By the time he got back from his trip, the book would be out and available in any bookstore."

"But the Angel of Death stepped in," whispered Tinney from the edge of her chair, "and that ended the matter."

"Elvira, did Jonathan explain why he felt so strongly about seeing the manuscript?"

"Alex's book is a *roman à clef*. One of the four main characters is clearly Jonathan. Alex knew Jonathan very well and for a long time. I suppose Jonathan was concerned about how Alex's book treated the character based on Jonathan."

"And how did he treat him?" Bogdanovic asked.

"Alex's portrait of the skunk is so perfectly realized that I joked with Alex about bracing himself for a Dodge libel suit."

"I think we'd better have a look at that book," Flynn said. "Do you have a copy we can take with us? If not, when could we have it picked up?"

Elvira rose behind the mound of paper. "Oh, my dear, that's not possible."

"Surely you have a photocopier on the premises?"

"Several. That is not the point. I simply cannot release the book to an unauthorized person prior to publication date."

"Elvira, this is a police matter," Bogdanovic said. "This is a *murder* case. You can hardly call us unauthorized persons."

"I'm sorry, dear boy. The only way I could possibly consider your request would be if you brought me a writ. Then I suppose our legal department would want to jump in."

"Elvira, this is silly."

"Sergeant, it is not silly! It's the old story. Government wants to look at what people who write are writing about. The Constitution says no. I say, 'God bless the First Amendment!' "

"This is not government interfering with the freedom of an author to write," Flynn said forcefully, "nor your freedom to publish. The contents of this book may shed light on why Dodge was murdered."

"I presume you're as interested in Dodge's murderer being brought to the bar of justice as we are," Bogdanovic said plaintively.

"I stand four-square for justice. But there is a principle at stake that I cannot brush aside on a personal whim. Should my legal department advise me to give you a copy of the book, then I will. But not before."

"Excuse me, please," whispered Margaret Tinney. "But I was thinking as I listened to you that if you feel you must know this instant what Alex wrote, who don't you just go and ask *him?*"

26

Tinker, Tailor, Soldier, Sailor

CHIEF OF DETECTIVES Harvey Goldstein rocked slowly in his chair. "These authors strike me as Lestrade and Gregson struck Sherlock Holmes in *A Study in Scarlet*," he said disdainfully. "He found the two Scotland Yard inspectors as jealous as a pair of professional beauties. But I don't see what you hope to find in Dodge's interest in Somerfield's manuscript that will contribute to wrapping up this case."

"Somerfield's book may turn out to be irrelevant," Bogdanovic answered. "But it was important enough to Dodge to harass Eveland about at the Edgars dinner and to make a date with her to see it Saturday morning of the day he was to leave the country. I know when I've got a big trip facing me, the last thing I want is business to transact a few hours before I'm due at the airport."

"Have you learned where Dodge was going?"

"Leibholz's search of his house turned up a ticket to London dated for Saturday and then open dates for points east."

"Do we know why he was traveling?"

"He said at the Edgars dinner that he was researching a new book. He also tweaked Wiggins about looking up the Wiggins family tree at the Public Records Office in London. My impression was that the Wiggins problem, as Dodge put it, was a sideshow."

Goldstein swung his chair to a position that afforded him the spectacular view from his window, then swung back. "If you want me to scrape up a judge to give you a paper to pry the book from Elvira Eveland's grasp, I'll do it. But she's got a real basis for squealing about infringing First Amendment rights. Do we need that fight? What about asking Somerfield for a copy of whatever he wrote that Dodge was so anxious about reading?"

"On the way here I phoned the marina to see if he was back from wherever he went on Saturday. I got a constant busy signal."

"This is Wednesday. Where do you go by boat for five days?"

"He could be anywhere on the north or south shore of Long Island. Down the Jersey coast. Maryland, Virginia, Florida. He has a place in Key West. Maybe he's running drugs. I could call our brethren in Narcotics to see if his name rings bells. Maybe we'll luck out and find they've got him under surveillance."

Goldstein shook his head. "Show me a drug dealer who wastes time writing books. He'd have to peddle a few hundred thousand copies to equal one kilo of cocaine."

Bogdanovic turned to Flynn. "Arlene, you're awfully quiet."

"I was thinking about Somerfield taking off like that. Not so much that he might have skipped town to avoid a murder charge, but if somehow he knew Dodge was dead and decided to make himself scarce for a while."

"Like the Clements kid? He vanished on Saturday."

"In his case, I think it was a matter of grab the goods and split. But in mulling over Somerfield's sudden departure, I wonder if he might have had the same experience as Griffith. A shot in the dark or something like it. Consider for a moment that we have three guys who write mystery books but who also were very close friends in the life they had before they started grinding out thrillers. One of them gets murdered and his body is dumped on the property of another, possibly to make him look culpable. When he's not immediately arrested, he barely misses being gunned down in his house. Isn't it possible that a similar attempt was made on Somerfield's life, that it failed, and that he departed post haste for a safer port? I'm still speculating. According to Eveland, Somerfield's book is a *roman à clef,* presumably in which Dodge and the others appear as thinly disguised characters. Why did that get Dodge so agitated? Is it too much to assume that if Dodge had been disturbed by the notion of being in Somerfield's novel, someone else might also have been?"

"Morgan Griffith?"

"But Griffith was a target. Twice. First with the body in the boathouse. Then a bullet through his window."

"Therefore, your scenario requires a fourth man," Goldstein

said, rocking slightly. "Any nominees, Arlene?"

As she shook her head, Bogdanovic almost leapt from his chair. "We can ask Griffith on our way back from seeing if Somerfield's boat has hove into view. Or is it hoven?"

A few minutes later as he started the car in the basement garage of One Police Plaza, she said, "How does that rhyme go? 'Tinker, tailor, soldier, spy.' "

"That's wrong, kiddo," Bogdanovic said. "It goes, 'Tinker, tailor, soldier, *sailor,* rich man, poor man, beggarman, thief.' "

She looked at him sidelong. "Not in John le Carré's novel."

"Sorry. I never read it."

"What about the television series? Surely you watched Alec Guinness as George Smiley?"

"Nope," he said, nosing the car onto the street.

"You *are* a hopeless mess. Goldstein is right about mystery stories. You *can* learn something from them."

He accelerated through a yellow light and headed toward the uptown ramp of the East River Drive. "What's your point?"

"According to Griffith, Alexander Somerfield's journalistic endeavors were a cover for espionage."

"Somerfield was a spook? I think he was putting you on."

"Why should he do that?"

"For the same reason he joined his pals in the fun at the Edgars dinner, stringing me along about how to murder Jonathan Dodge and get away with it. If you ask me, all the people we've met in this case have bats in the belfry. Kooks. Each and every one of 'em. I wouldn't be surprised if they all had a part in offing Dodge. Hell, if they'd asked me, I might have joined in the conspiracy. The man was—pardon the expression, but there's no other one—a prick. I wouldn't be a bit surprised if whoever did it gets a special Edgar Allan Poe Award the next time these loons throw a dinner. So, please, can we forget this 'tinker, tailor, spy' baloney and concentrate on what this case comes down to? Murder plain and simple for one of the tried and true motives that have kept you and me gainfully employed."

"Money, love, revenge."

"With money the front runner by far," he said, swinging into the fast lane. "As Richard Nixon advised, 'Follow the money.' "

"There's not been a hint of money as motive in this case."

"I've only been on it since Monday."

"A day behind me."

Hard light glinting off the flaked surface of the East River caused her to lower the passenger visor. He slipped on aviator sunglasses.

"Johnny, how come you've never expressed interest in visiting the scene of the crime?"

"Why should I go way out in the sticks when you already gave it the once-over? Besides, the boathouse was not the scene of the crime. Jonathan Dodge took his big leap into eternity right here in little old New York."

"He didn't leap," Flynn snapped. "He was shoved. At the point of a sword."

PART SIX

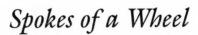
Any spoke will lead an ant to the hub.

—Nero Wolfe

27

Scarlet Thread of Murder

THE FLASHING ROOF LIGHTS of three patrol cars whipped arcs of red across dozens of white boats moored between long jetties and linking gangways against the gray background of the wide, swift Hudson River. "Oh God, let this be something else!" Flynn cried, as she bounded from the car and dashed toward Somerfield's boat, knowing it was not.

Below deck, face down beside a bunkbed, the corpse was clad in a short-sleeved white terrycloth shirt, navy blue shorts, and yellow canvas deck shoes. The grayed head twisted slightly to the left in a halo of congealed blood.

Beside the body stood Lieutenant Michael Borrero. Tall, slim, and elegant in the blue and gold braid of his rank, he had to bend slightly to keep from bumping his head on the ceiling. With only a nod of greeting to Bogdanovic, he said, "The kid who works here told me he found the body when he came on board to deliver a card to Somerfield. Imagine my surprise when I saw the name on it was my friend and colleague Sergeant Johnny Bogdanovic of the Chief of Detectives' office. Care to say why you wanted to see him?"

Bogdanovic crouched beside the body. "We thought he might be a material witness."

Borrero greeted Flynn by touching two fingers to the shiny black visor of his blue cap. "Is this a new partner?"

"Chief Investigator Arlene Flynn," she said, bending over the corpse. "Stone County D.A. squad. When did you get the call?"

"About fifteen minutes ago. But the kid who found him says the boat docked sometime during the night when he was off duty. Throat's cut. We won't know if he was also stabbed till the M.E.

gets here and turns him over. We haven't found anything that looks like the weapon."

"You won't," she said.

Bogdanovic rose. "Mickey, you'll be getting official orders from the Chief assigning this homicide to me. Meanwhile, we'd appreciate getting a copy of your report and anything else your people turn up. As soon as possible, please."

"In case you haven't already discovered it, Arlene, around the department this guy you're working with is known as 'A.S.A.P. John,' " said the lieutenant as she and Bogdanovic climbed to the deck. "But in this case, given the crime scene, maybe it should be 'Full-speed-ahead-and-damn-the-torpedoes Bogdanovic.' "

As Borrero chuckled at his joke and they stepped onto the dock, she said urgently, "If anything's to be done a.s.a.p. in this damn case, Johnny, it's letting Griffith know about what happened here and making certain that he doesn't suffer the fate of Dodge and Somerfield. Then, by God in heaven, you and I are going to find out what made them into a triumvirate that somebody suddenly wants to kill off one by one, besides their penchant for stringing words together in clever little puzzles between book covers."

"Have you considered the possibility that we're dealing with a nutty dissatisfied reader? One who's tired of figuring out who done it long before all the suspects are brought together in one room to listen to the detective explain how he solved it. If so, the jury could well return a verdict of justifiable homicide."

"In different circumstances, John, that *might* be funny," Flynn said as they reached the car. "Now it's in bad taste."

"You're right. I apologize. Do you have Griffith's number? I'll try to raise him on my cellular and advise him to lock his door and stay put till we get there."

Watching him punch the number pad on the hand-held phone, she shook her head in wonder at the advances in technology since she became a police officer. When the call went unanswered, she seized the phone. "Let me try the Traitor's Lair number. And pray he's there."

28

Requiem for Cold Warriors

GRIFFITH SANK HEAVILY into the Chesterfield couch.

"Alex murdered too?" he murmured, pounding his knees with his fists. Staring down at the Oriental carpet, he sighed. "Alex was with me when I bought that rug in Pakistan. He, Jonathan, and I were in Peshawar in 1985 trying to get across the border into Afghanistan to cover the war in which the rebel Mujahideen were kicking the Russians' ass." He looked up with a smile. "Alex got us through the Khyber Pass disguised as Muslims. He had a flair for pulling off stunts like that. He got me a fantastic deal on this rug. If I'd tried to buy it on my own I would have been royally fleeced." Moist eyes searched the detectives' grim faces. "Will you please tell me what the hell is going on with these murders?"

Flynn sat in the green wingback chair. "We hope you may be able to help us find out."

Leaning on the mantel, Bogdanovic said, "We'd like you to go over your personal history with Dodge and Somerfield."

Griffith fished in the pocket of the blue sweater he had worn on Sunday and withdrew the pipe he had smoked that blustery afternoon. "I see where you're coming from." He tapped the bit of the gracefully curved stem against his forehead. "You think the motive for these murders and the attempt on my life might lie buried somewhere in the experiences I shared with Jonathan and Alex way back when."

"We'd be fools to ignore the possibility," Flynn said.

Lowering the cold pipe to his mouth, he sucked it as if it were lit. "That's a whole lot of water under the bridge. You are talking decades. All the way back to the mid-sixties."

"Start then," she said. "You told me you met Jonathan when you both got jobs in a television network news department. When did you meet Somerfield?"

"That was spring of 1966," Griffith said as he pulled a tobacco pouch from the other pocket of the sweater. "Jonathan and I were having dinner with another newsman, Gene Valentine, in the . . ."

" . . . The man I saw in the photograph in your apartment?"

"That's him. Gene was a freelancer. He peddled stories to a news syndicate. He, Jonathan, and I were in the restaurant on the roof of the Caravelle Hotel in Saigon when Jonathan pointed out Somerfield and told me Alex's real purpose in being in Vietnam was not to report on the war. He said that was cover for Alex's work in intelligence. Alex was an agent of influence."

"Excuse me. What's that?"

Fingering a clump of tobacco into the pipe bowl caked with the ash of countless smokings, Griffith said, "The common picture of an intelligence agent is of a dashing James Bond type tangling with enemy spies and carrying a license to kill. But the duties of an agent of influence are different."

He struck a wooden match and lit the pipe.

"An agent of influence is a spycraft term. It refers to an agent who attempts to foster a climate, an atmosphere, favorable to his side or harmful to the enemy. Alex's job was to plant good news items. He schmoozed with correspondents and reported back on the gossipy stuff—who was romancing whom, who might be set up to be compromised by one of the true James Bond types, who in the press corps might be enticed to put pro-war spins on stories. And who among the war correspondents ought to be added to the government enemies list. That included anybody who wasn't all-out and gung-ho behind U.S. policy. There were not all that many in 1966. The anti-war sentiment among the reporters in Vietnam did not jell until after the Red offensive in early 1968. Incidentally, that Tet holiday operation by the Commies was not the defeat for our side it was made to be by the press and the anti-war movement. The Viet Cong and North Vietnamese Army got their asses kicked. The perception was otherwise in the news coverage. Anyway, after the Tet Offensive many in the press corps in-country turned against the war, just as they did here at home. Some of them also turned on Somerfield. Eventually, he departed Vietnam. So did I, by the way, although his leaving had nothing to do with my going. We both wound up in Moscow."

"Valentine and Dodge stayed behind?"

Discovering the pipe had gone out, Griffith struck another match to it and puffed several times before satisfying himself it was lit. "Jonathan spent a lot of his time after Tet hanging around with the Saigon police. As I said, in his chest beat the heart of a police reporter. That's when he discovered the intrepid cop he later wrote about in *Incident on Tu Do Street*. That was Saigon's main drag. All the posh shops, bars, and whorehouses were located along Tu Do Street. The detective was investigating the murder of a Vietnamese whose body was found in the men's room of a bar with the throat slit. The murder became an obsession for the cop. It also consumed Jonathan's attention. When nothing came of it after a few months, Jonathan turned up in Moscow."

"Did Somerfield continue as an agent of influence there?"

Griffith wiped dirty fingers on the sweater. "I doubt that. It was too risky. Soviet-American relations were in a deep freeze at the time. It wasn't till Nixon came into the White House that things warmed up. I believe Alex had been given other tasks by his controllers. If, indeed, he was still an active agent at that time."

"Back to Saigon for a minute," Bogdanovic said. "If Dodge knew Somerfield was an agent and passed that information on to you and Valentine . . ."

"Gene already knew it. All the Vietnam hands knew."

"So how effective could Somerfield have been if his cover had been blown?"

"The press corps liked Alex. He came across like the whore with a golden heart. He could be extremely useful. If you needed an airlift to get you into the boondocks to cover the action, he had ways of getting you a helicopter. That chopper ride let Alex report to Washington that he'd locked you up as a client."

"Even though it wasn't true?"

"Remember, this was the war in which they routinely faked the enemy body count. And our own. The only reporter I knew who got upset about Alex's antics was Valentine. But that was years later, when we were all in Jerusalem covering the aftermath of the

Israeli defeat of the Arabs in the 1973 Yom Kippur War. Gene had a run-in with Alex smack in the middle of the lobby of the King David Hotel. He chewed Alex out, up, and down for reporting back to Washington in 1968 that he'd bought Valentine's loyalty. But, of course, Alex had lied."

Flynn asked, "It took Valentine all that time from Vietnam in 1968 to Israel in 1973 to upbraid Somerfield for it?"

"I guess Gene didn't know it before then. Jonathan and I had to jump in and pull them apart. Then Gene flew off the handle at Jonathan *and* me. I don't recall his talking to us again. In fact, I haven't seen Gene to talk to since then. We did cross paths a couple of times, including running into one another in Peshawar. I tried to buy him a coffee in Dean's Hotel. He walked out. The last time I saw him was at the British Airways arrivals terminal at Kennedy Airport a couple of weeks ago. But he breezed right past me without a word. I had no idea he was in New York. My God, could he be the one? Why should Gene pick now to settle scores?"

"Did you know that Somerfield was about to come out with a new novel that Elvira Eveland was editing?" Flynn asked.

"Alex always had some work in progress. But he was always so secretive. He never talked with me about what he was up to. Nor anyone else, save for Elvira. Jonathan had the soul of a police reporter. Alex had the soul of a spy. That is what made Alex's cloak-and-dagger thrillers such compelling page-turners. They reek of verisimilitude!"

"Evidently, Dodge knew about the new book," Flynn said. "He tried to coerce Eveland into showing him the manuscript."

Griffith chewed the pipe stem. "Is that so? Did she?"

Bogdanovic grunted. "That battleax wouldn't even let us see them. She told us to get a writ!"

Griffith puffed a smoke ring. "That's Elvira, all right! She may look as docile as Whistler's mother, but she's a tough lady."

"As a friend of both Dodge and Somerfield, and from your perspective as an author," said Flynn, "do you have any ideas as to why Dodge would be so insistent on reading Somerfield's manuscript? Could he have been afraid that the book had something in it about him that was embarrassing?"

"Jonathan was primarily a nonfiction author; Alex's genre was the spy novel. But a *roman à clef* based on Alex's experiences as an agent would be of interest to everyone who knew him. That includes Jonathan. Certainly, Valentine would be."

"At the dinner, Dodge said he was researching a new book. Do you happen to know his subject?"

"Sergeant, Jonathan could be just as tight-lipped as Alex. He was one of those authors who believe that talking about their books kills the urge to write them. Others, like me, blab away all the time. I find it helps me to think through plots."

"Jonathan seemed to delight in the prospect of coming back from his overseas research junket with information that would be of interest to everyone at the dinner. He looked at you and said something about a question of identity."

"He may have been looking at me, but he was directing his words to Wiggins. The phrase 'question of identity' was a pointed reference to his intention to investigate the origins of Wiggins's name. 'A Case of Identity' is the title of a Sherlock Holmes story. Jonathan liked being cryptic. He found pleasure in making people wonder about him. That's why he worked hard at fashioning a persona. The opera cape. Walking sticks. The grand entrance. The dramatic exit. The provocative after-dinner speech. He got a kick out of stirring things up. Forcing people to pay attention to him. When he was carrying on a campaign among members of the Baker Street Irregulars to obtain an investiture, I suggested to him that because he found such delight in forcing people to prance to his tune, his investiture ought to be 'The Dancing Men.' He was not amused."

"Did he get an investiture?"

"Given his well-known habit of suing people, or threatening to, he received the investiture of the litigious Mr. Frankland in *The Hound of the Baskervilles*. It thoroughly delighted him."

"Did Somerfield have an investiture?"

"Alex was not a member of the BSI."

"What about you?"

"I'm thrilled to be another character from *The Hound*. I am Selden, the Notting Hill murderer. However, I hasten to add that the only murders you can charge me with are those I committed in my novels. The scene of my crimes is over there by the window. My word processor."

"Considering what came through that glass the other night," Flynn said, peering across the library, "I suggest you move it."

"It's on the agenda that brought me here today. I've also got to call Jeb Fulmer to see about having the pane replaced and plugging the hole in the wall where the bullet hit. Or should I leave it? Do you suppose the ghosts would object?"

Bogdanovic's eyes went wide. "Ghosts?"

"Miss Flynn informed me I bought a haunted house." Noticing the pipe had gone out once again, he returned it to a pocket. "Have you discerned anything in the experiences I shared with Jonathan and Alex that might be of help to you?"

"A little more data on Gene Valentine would be helpful," Flynn said.

"I'm afraid I've given you all I remember. Gene was also a man who kept his own counsel. Other than the fact that he was one of the gang of reporters who showed up at all the Cold War crisis spots, I knew nothing about him. Jonathan would know. Or Alex might . . . be . . . able . . . ."

As Griffith's voice choked and his words faded, Flynn heard a distant chirping of birds and thought they might be in the trees clustered around the boathouse.

"In view of these murders and the shot taken at you," said Bogdanovic gently, "and considering all that you've told us today about this man Valentine, I'm going to recommend to my boss that you be given around-the-clock police protection."

"Please don't, Sergeant B. I'd feel uncomfortable. Like most authors, I'm a solitary guy. I wouldn't get any work done."

"You are, of course, free to do as you wish," Flynn said as she rose from the wingback. "But I do hope you'll agree that two dead authors in less than a week have been quite enough."

"Thanks for the concern. But I'll be just fine."

29

Location, Location, Location

"WHEN YOU BROUGHT US this case, Arlene," said Goldstein as he rubbed his pointy chin. "I thought it would unfold like a Jane Marple story, or maybe a Hercule Poirot. One of these neat little mysteries involving civilized, cultured people who commit murder for all the customary reasons and conclude with the solution explained over tea and crumpets in an English flower garden. Now you and Johnny are telling me the plot may have been ripped from *The Spy Who Came In from the Cold.*"

"You're no more astonished than I am, Chief," Flynn said.

Goldstein rocked back in his chair. "I get damn impatient with spy stories. You never seem to get straightforward clues."

"We're not without them," Bogdanovic said laconically as he settled into his customary deep chair. "We still have to hear from Forensics about the sword stick, from the state police lab on the items they removed from the boathouse, and from Borrero's going-over of Somerfield's boat. Somewhere in all of that there's bound to be a lead. And Al and Red are still out combing the city for Clements."

"I'm less hopeful about that angle now that this new player has popped up. This Gene Valentine. I could see how the kid might know something about Dodge's murder. Or even that he did it. But if Valentine did Dodge and Somerfield, how does the kid fit in?"

"Maybe he was used by Valentine to get to Dodge. Valentine could have gotten to Somerfield through Dodge. Once these deeds were done, the little Judas collected his thirty pieces of silver and split."

"That's possible," Flynn said as she drummed fingers on the

arms of her chair. "But if that were it, why would Clements try to peddle Dodge's prized first edition to Wiggins?"

"Greed," Bogdanovic replied. "Don't forget, he cleaned out that house of everything he could tote away and sell."

"I'll keep an open mind on that, Johnny," she said. "But I think it's more likely that he went on the run because he'd been frightened off."

Bogdanovic's nose crinkled as though it smelled a bad odor. "Frightened by what?"

"If Dodge's murder took place in the house late Friday night or early Saturday morning," she said, "he might have had the bad luck to have been an inadvertent but unnoticed eyewitness."

Bogdanovic wrenched himself out of his slouch. "Why 'if' it took place in the house? Where else could he have been killed?"

Flynn rose and crossed the office to the windows with their view of the city and the East River. "What is it they say about the three most important factors in succeeding in business? 'Location, location, location.' I am bothered by location. The location of Clements at this moment bothers me. The location of the murder bothers me. The location where the body was discovered has bothered me all along. *And* I am bothered by how it got from the one to the other. How do you transport a corpse through Manhattan without attracting attention?"

Goldstein laughed. "You *have* been away from the city a long time, Arlene. It seems to be done with a sickening regularity."

"I've also been perplexed by the timing of two events. One is the activity of Jimmy Clements on Saturday. The other is the departure of Somerfield's boat from the marina, also on Saturday. Where did he go? Why? Did he go away by himself? Or did he have the pleasure of someone's company?"

"Such as Clements?" Goldstein said. "Valentine?"

Flynn returned to her chair. "We also do not know if Somerfield was killed upon returning to the marina or before the boat came in. It could have been either. Had the murderer been aboard *Karla?* Or did he lie in wait?"

"How we answer these questions will carry this investigation in very different directions," Goldstein interjected.

"Assuming a conspiracy between Somerfield and Valentine to

kill their old friend," she continued, "I can see the following happening. Somerfield lured Dodge to the boat, where he and Gene Valentine murdered him on Friday night shortly after the MWA dinner. Their motive is anybody's guess at the moment. Perhaps it lies buried in the events Griffith described for us. Somerfield then attended the party at the Usual Suspects."

"Leaving Valentine aboard to make sure nobody discovered Dodge's body," Bogdanovic picked up. "Upon Somerfield's return, they sailed up the Hudson to Traitor's Lair and deposited the corpse in Morgan Griffith's boathouse. They knew he wasn't there—he was at the dinner. It was also a dark and stormy night, so they had no fear of being seen when they docked."

"Because the boathouse's jetty has a roof," Flynn said, "Dodge's tuxedo remained dry."

"They boated back down to the city. Valentine paid a call at Gramercy Park to leave the cape and the walking stick as a ruse to make it appear that Dodge had gone home after the dinner."

"That seems to fit this scenario."

"Wait a minute. Dodge's house key was on the body. How did Valentine get in?"

Goldstein grunted. "Johnny, come on! This is a spy story."

"Okay, he broke in," said Bogdanovic with a shrug. "Or the kid let him in. He would if he were in on the plot."

"That's a possibility," Flynn said. "But for now let's not assume it. In the morning Somerfield and Valentine went away on the boat, reason unknown, and then returned after they learned of the discovery of the body through news reports. But what Somerfield did not know was that Valentine had also marked him for murder. Once *Karla* was back at her berth, Valentine slit his throat and went on his merry way. Assuming Jimmy Clements was not in on the murder, he would have returned to Dodge's house after spending Friday night out. I can't see someone with his looks and known as Jimmy Climax sitting home while his lover is out for the evening, can you? Perhaps he found the cape and sword, maybe he didn't."

"But on Saturday morning something led him to believe Dodge would never be coming home," Flynn went on. "Only he can tell us what put that notion in his head. The last time he was heard of is noon Saturday at the Usual Suspects in possession of a rare book.

Which is why I do not believe he was part of a conspiracy to kill Dodge. If he had been, I doubt that the man who had murdered twice would be in a frame of mind to spare the life of a kid who could either blackmail him or turn state's witness against him, should it come to that eventuality."

"How goes the hunt for this kid, Johnny?" Goldstein asked. "What've you heard from Al and Red?"

"So far, zilch."

"You've heard zilch? Or they've come up with zilch?"

"The search has been fruitless. Excuse the double entendre."

30

Naked City

IN THE TERMINOLOGY of police, Detectives Leibholz and Reiter had spent two nights staking out the East Fifty-third Street bar called the Round-a-Lay on the basis of "information and belief" that sooner or later Jimmy Clements might appear there. They learned this from a confidential informant adorned with a Dolly Parton wig and a slinky silver-sequined gown. She used the name Sybil Vane, although Leibholz and Reiter knew her as Anthony Mitchell and half a dozen other aliases on a departmental rap sheet that had been started fifteen years earlier when Anthony was fourteen.

"Round-a-Lay caters to the *chichi* cly-ahn-*tell* that suits Jimmy's taste for men of an older generation who are superbly endowed in their wallets," he had explained in the dressing room he shared with seven other drag queens in the basement of the Strip World Show Palace on Eighth Avenue—cusp of the Midtown universe of glamorous Broadway that once upon a time had been Sybil Vane's dream. "What's the naughty child done to warrant the attentions of two of the city's finest plainclothes detectives? I thought you two *eschewed* working Vice long ago for Homicide. Don't tell me Jimmy's finally killed somebody!"

"You said that as if you'd expected him to," Reiter said.

"Everyone who knows Jimmy Climax expects it. He may be long where it counts, but Jimmy's temper has a very short fuse. He may not look it, what with his bedroom eyes and fake sweet sixteen innocence, but he can be dangerous if he thinks he's cornered. Take that as a word of friendly advice, gentlemen."

"Thanks for the info and the warning, Sybil," Leibholz said.

"And we do appreciate in advance your not telling Jimmy, should you see him before we do, that we're looking for him."

Sybil primped the mountainous platinum-hued wig. "Oh, he never comes around here anymore. Jimmy quit the dancing gig and the hustling the minute he latched onto a famous author with a town house in Gramercy Park. He's probably in Paris or L.A. or wherever rich writers go."

Emerging from the dark theater into midday glare, Leibholz said, "Obviously Sybil doesn't keep up with the news of the day."

Two nights later, peering across Fifty-third Street at the door of the Round-a-Lay in the hope that Jimmy Climax had returned to his former ways, he said, "When you and I worked Vice, I used to go off a shift feeling disgusted by all that we saw. Now I feel sorry for people like Sybil. Back then all they had to worry them if they turned a trick was coming down with a dose of clap. Today, it could be a dose of death called AIDS."

At four in the morning a brutish-looking middle-aged man they knew as a soldier in the Guido Perillo crime family, who both owned the bar and served as its bouncer, shut the door and padlocked it. Reiter yawned and stretched. "Where to now, partner? The after-hours spots in the Village? The cruising streets in Chelsea? The trucks of the West Side docks? Or do you agree with me that we are wasting our time and that this kid has headed out for parts unknown? Atlantic City, maybe. Down to Miami. Out to the Coast, like Sybil said. Las Vegas. Maybe he's already in bed with Dodge's replacement. For all we know, you and I have been eating sandwiches and guzzling coffee while the object of our endeavors has been sipping champagne and scoffing down beluga caviar in a plush pad on Sutton Place."

"You may be right about that. But he hasn't had the warmth of companionship I've enjoyed," Leibholz said with a chuckle. "In case he's not shacked up in comfort, let's take one more spin around the city that never sleeps."

Starting the engine, Reiter muttered, "Look out, Naked City! Here come Leibholz and Reiter."

At six o'clock, Leibholz said, "Let's call it quits. Head for the Empire Diner. Breakfast is on me."

Forty-five miles north, the click of a clock radio woke Flynn a second before the mellow voice of Paul Smith on all-news station WINS warned her to expect a sultry day in the city.

Dressed for the heat in a light, powder blue pants suit, she found District Attorney Aaron Benson coatless at his desk, the sleeves of a green shirt folded to his elbows. He was bent over a two-page typewritten document. Sitting opposite him, she resisted an urge to blurt that he looked as cool as a cucumber.

"I do not envy you being in the city today, Arlene. They say it's going to be a scorcher down there," he said, picking up the papers and handing them to her. "The state police crime scene analysis report came in late yesterday. I saw nothing in it that I felt you needed to know right away. Lots of footprints in mud and some liftable fingerprints, all of which belong to Fulmer and Griffith. Nothing remarkable about Dodge's clothing, either. No holes, rips, or tears. The tuxedo had been dry-cleaned recently. There were lots of variously colored fibers stuck to it, front and back. The report suggests the body was probably wrapped in a blanket or quilt or something similar while being transported."

"If he was brought on Somerfield's boat, the fibers could be from a deckchair throw. I must say, it never crossed my mind when we were in the boathouse on Sunday that the body might have been brought in by way of the jetty. I focused totally on the front door."

"The body *was* just inside. The jetty was yards away. Shall I send the crime scene team back to give the place another going-over?"

"It couldn't hurt. Though with all the rain that night, I doubt if they'll find anything. But if you can spare someone from your squad to talk to people with houses on the river in the vicinity of Traitor's Lair, they might turn up someone who saw the boat."

"I'll spring Dick Green and Miles Mander. What's on tap for you today in Goldstein territory?"

Stuffing the crime scene report in her purse, Flynn said, "I'm hoping we'll get the NYPD reports on Dodge's house, the possible murder weapon, and the going-over that Somerfield's boat got. I'm also waiting for a warrant to let me see a copy of Somerfield's latest book. And we're still looking for Jimmy Clements."

"I gather from your telephoned briefing yesterday that you are now disregarding as suspects those who were at the dinner, and will be concentrating on the late entry in the field."

"I haven't ruled all of them out. But Valentine has, indeed, come from out of nowhere to lead the pack. A dark horse if ever there were one."

"If anyone had told me when we were slipping and sliding in the mud on Sunday that by the end of the week we'd be investigating the murder of a secret agent, I'd have had him committed forthwith to the county mental hospital!"

31

A Bit of Deduction

"I'M SORRY TO START YOUR DAY with bad news, Arlene," Bogdanovic said, poking his head into her borrowed office. "But I just got off the horn with Peterson in Forensics. He informed me that the technician who's handling the tests on the sword cane called in sick. He'll be back tomorrow. That's the earliest we can have his report."

"Damn! Can't somebody else do it?"

"They've all got cases of their own."

"How many are working a double homicide?"

"I know you're disappointed. So am I. But how would you feel if you were a detective waiting for one of those lab wizards to solve your case for you and you found out he was being yanked off it and reassigned? We get more than two thousand homicides a year dumped on our lab people. Believe it or not, even though they're scientists, they're human. Sometimes they get sick. But there is a bright spot. Borrero is waiting for us in Goldstein's office."

They found the lieutenant wearing a blue seersucker suit.

"You were right about not finding the weapon, Arlene," he said, holding a sheaf of crime report forms. "I even brought in divers to search the river bottom. It was a knife we were looking for, by the way. The medical examiner says it was probably made of plastic, small enough to tuck into a sleeve or conceal easily in the hand. Or the kind that a commando might carry in the top of his boot. Judging from the wound, it was double-edged and sharp as a razor, curved up to form a ridge in the middle. Not exactly a knife you'd find in a galley drawer or a fisherman's tackle box. This thing was brought onto that boat, presumably for the purpose it fulfilled."

"Did your men come across any blankets?" Flynn asked. "Any of those throws people cover their legs with when lounging on deck? The state police lab reported finding a quantity of colored fibers adhering to Dodge's tuxedo that could have come from such a blanket."

Borrero scanned an inventory. "There were lots of big beach towels. A couple of straw mats. A bunch of cushions of various sizes, shapes, and colors. Ah, here you go: 'Four blankets, Navajo style.' Nothing about what colors they were. But those things are usually pretty elaborate."

"Where are the fibers from the tuxedo?" Goldstein asked. "We can compare them to these blankets."

"I can have them sent down in a couple of hours at most."

"Please do. Johnny, set up the tests. And tell the lab that this time *I'm* the one telling them we want a report a.s.a.p."

Flynn muttered, "Good luck."

"Beg pardon?" Goldstein said.

"Nothing at all, Chief," she said while Bogdanovic grinned.

Borrero continued, "We talked to everyone we could find who was at the marina when Somerfield's boat pulled in, but nobody paid any attention. Not that there were many who could have if they wanted to. The marina was pretty well buttoned up for the night. The man who was on duty in the office said the boat docked at its usual slip and no one got on or off during his shift. That was between eleven p.m. and seven in the morning. The guy who took over for him also saw nothing out of the ordinary."

"How did he define 'ordinary'?"

"Things got busy in the morning. Lots of people were coming and going between seven and the time the kid who found the body went on board to deliver Johnny's card."

"Therefore, the killer could have been on board all night long, then slipped away under cover of later comings and goings."

"That's a possibility."

"What about fingerprints?" Goldstein asked.

"If we dusted the *QE2* we couldn't have come up with more than we found on *Karla*. Bring in Somerfield's murderer and maybe we'll find a match."

"Highly unlikely," Flynn said. "A man who carries a plastic

knife of the kind you described is not going to leave prints."

"Anything else, Mickey?"

"We ran a check for ship-to-shore radio traffic and Somerfield's cellular phone use. No activity."

"Did you find any indication that someone was aboard *Karla* for any length of time, besides Somerfield? Two sets of dishes, for instance? Two bunks slept in? That sort of thing."

"I do a little boating myself, Arlene. *Karla* was as shipshape as the day Somerfield bought her."

"Do you know when that was?"

"Five years ago. Paid for in cash."

"Could *Karla* possibly have been used in running drugs?"

Borrero chuckled. "That did occur to me, so I had Narcotics turn a sniffer dog loose. Clean as a whistle. In my opinion, *Karla* has never been employed in the drug trade. And from what I know about her skipper, Somerfield did not fit the profile. If he'd been around during Prohibition, he might have made a pretty dashing rum runner. But drugs? Nah."

Goldstein asked, "Anything else, Arlene?"

"Only to thank the lieutenant for a very thorough briefing and a fine investigation."

Goldstein's eyes turned to Bogdanovic. "Johnny?"

He shook his head.

Leaving the office, Borrero paused at the door. "There's one thing still outstanding. We're surveying cab and car services, in case the killer hired wheels to get him the hell out of there. If anything promising turns up, I'll give you all a whistle."

As the door closed behind him, Flynn asked, "What are we to make of the knife that appears to have been used to slit Somerfield's throat?"

"Highly specialized, I'd say," Bogdanovic replied.

"Such as an intelligence agent might possess?"

"Is it your suggestion that Somerfield was killed with his own knife?"

"That's one possibility. The other is that Gene Valentine, if that's who killed Somerfield, may have been more than Griffith supposed him to be."

"Are you implying that Jonathan Dodge was also an agent and

that Valentine was settling some old grievance among spooks?"

"Not at all. But how did Dodge earn his livelihood?"

"He wrote True Crime books."

"Quite right, Johnny," Goldstein said. "And damn good ones, too. But Dodge also wrote about *spies*. I read one of them. It was an anecdotal history of Cold War espionage. He entitled it, uh, wait a minute, the name's at the tip of my tongue."

"Secrets of Lubyanka," Flynn said.

Goldstein banged a fist on his desk. "Right!"

Bogdanovic fretted. "What the hell is Lubyanka?"

"It was the name of a Czarist prison in Moscow that became the headquarters of Soviet Intelligence. The KGB."

"Or as it used to be known in the good old days of the Cold War," Goldstein said with a widening smile, "the *dreaded* KGB."

Bogdanovic shifted uneasily in his deep chair. "I know I'm practically illiterate by your standards. . . ."

Goldstein guffawed. *"Practically?"*

"There is nothing in what we've come to know about Dodge, except that book, that in any way points to his being remotely connected with cloak-and-dagger stuff. If Dodge had been a spy, I think Griffith would have known it. Or suspected it. And if Dodge were a spook, why would he expose Somerfield as one?"

"I don't believe Dodge was a spook," Flynn said. "But isn't it possible that the new book he was working on was a return to the subject of *Secrets of Lubyanka?* Consider it. He was on his way out of the country, going to London and points east. Before leaving, he felt an urgent need to take a peek at Somerfield's new book. And what do we know of the subject matter of the book?"

"Blessed little."

"We know it's a *roman à clef.* Given the fact that Somerfield was a novelist specializing in the spy genre, and a real ex-spy to boot, is it too much to suppose that Dodge suspected *Valentine* was also an agent and hoped Somerfield's book would confirm it?"

"Explain how Valentine learned all this."

"The man was a lifelong journalist. He might have heard via the old boys' grapevine. He could have picked up gossip. Imagine Valentine getting these inklings that Somerfield might be about to expose his secret. He calls Dodge and plays the role of one old hand who covered the hot spots of the Cold War proposing a get together for old times' sake. One in which they'd bury the hatchet. After all, the United States and the Soviet Union did it. Why shouldn't a trio of aging scribblers do the same?"

"Accepting your theory for the purpose of discussion only, how come Griffith wasn't invited to this touching class reunion? If Valentine had set his mind on killing people out of his past, why wouldn't he take care of all three at once?"

"He wanted Griffith as a fall guy. We have been assuming that Dodge was killed in his house Friday night and Somerfield later in the week aboard *Karla*. Suppose they both were killed on the boat on Friday night. Valentine then took *Karla* up the river to Traitor's Lair to deposit Dodge's body in Griffith's boathouse. He returns to the marina for the night, staying on the boat, and then takes *Karla* out on Saturday morning, giving the impression it was Somerfield. Only Somerfield was below deck, dead of a cut throat. A few days later, Valentine brings *Karla* in and leaves us to conclude that Dodge and Somerfield were murdered at different times. In the meantime, Valentine has had the pleasure of having put Griffith on the hot seat and given himself plenty of time to disappear while the police concentrated on Griffith. When he saw Griffith hadn't been arrested, he decided to go up to Traitor's Lair and get rid of him. The shot missed. A dog barked. He fled."

"Hold it! How did Dodge's cape and cane get into the house?"

"Dodge left them there when he met Valentine before going up to the marina for the reunion with Somerfield. Dodge had to have gone *somewhere* after the Edgars dinner. We know he didn't go to the party at the Usual Suspects. I don't think he wandered around the streets in a rainstorm."

"I've got you there, I think. Dodge's tuxedo was dry when the body was found. He wasn't wearing his cape. But he had to go from Gramercy Park to Seventy-ninth Street in pouring rain and then onto the boat. He must have gotten soaked."

"Ever hear of an umbrella?"

Goldstein blared a laugh. "Whatever little bit of rain got on him would have dried by the time Valentine lugged the body into the boathouse, wrapped in something, probably one of Somerfield's blankets."

"And the umbrella?"

"Tossed overboard sometime during the cruise."

"That weekend boat ride puzzles me."

"Valentine probably figured that if Dodge's body were found immediately, somebody was likely to come round to the marina to question Somerfield. As you and I did, although not right away."

Goldstein exclaimed, "Arlene, that's a wonderful demonstration of deductive reasoning."

Bogdanovic rose from his chair. "Borrowing a line that I've heard in God knows how many detective stories, there's one thing I still do not understand. What's your explanation now for the activities of Jimmy Clements?"

Flynn tugged her lip. "I don't follow you."

"If Valentine met Dodge at the house after the dinner, where was Clements?"

"Knowing Dodge would be out late, Clements went out, too."

"Your previous theory to explain Clements's activities the next day was based on his possibly having been a witness to the murder. That was the basis for your reasoning as to why the kid tried to peddle the book to Wiggins. If he was out, how could he have been a witness? If he didn't witness the murder, then how did he know it was safe for him to loot the house? And don't ask me to believe that on the morning after the night Dodge happened to get murdered the kid finally got the bright idea to rip him off. You find it hard to believe in murder conspiracies. Well, I find it just as hard to accept coincidences in my murder cases."

"It's possible I'm wrong about the murder not having been committed in the house. We won't know for sure until we get the lab report, will we? Why Clements did what he did isn't going to be known for sure until Al and Red find him."

Amused by the verbal fencing, Goldstein looked at his watch. "Where the hell are those guys, by the way?"

"I assume they're asleep," Bogdanovic said. "They were up all night looking for the elusive Jimmy Climax. Al left word on my voice mail telling me they'll be in around one o'clock."

"Well, get hold of him and tell him that he and his partner should meet us at that hour at Neary's. They can report on their obvious failures over lunch. I'm buying."

Bogdanovic picked up the phone.

"Being of Irish lineage, Arlene," Goldstein said while Bogdanovic dialed, "you'll love Neary's. It's been my favorite eating place since it opened in 1968. It's charming! Totally New York, yet Irish. The owner, Jimmy Neary, is a leprechaun."

32

Something to Chew On

OFFERING A MEAT-AND-POTATOES bill of fare, Neary's occupied a small gray building on Fifty-seventh Street a block from Sutton Place. Immediately to their right as they entered was a long bar. Halfway down it, Leibholz and Reiter were laughing with a short, ruddy-faced, boyish-looking man with reddish curly hair who stood between them, his hands on their shoulders. With a glance at the door, he said loudly, "Heads up, fellas, here comes your boss."

Beyond the bar, candles flickered in frosted glass holders on red-clothed tables down the middle of the room and along wood-paneled walls festooned with vistas of Irish castles and photos presented to the proprietor by the Irish princes of American and New York politics.

As Neary sat them at a large, round corner table, a waitress with a red blouse and a black skirt and the lilting tones of Ireland in her voice presented menus.

"Please handle these with care, folks," Goldstein declared. "When they wear out, the proprietor gets fresh ones printed and the prices go up."

Laughing, Neary squeezed Goldstein's shoulder. "It's too late, Chief. The new ones are due in next week."

Scanning the photographs, Flynn saw that Senator Edward M. Kennedy had signed his "Ted." Not to be outdone, the late Thomas P. O'Neill, former Speaker of the U.S. House of Representatives, had penned: "May the wind be always at your back. Love, Tip." A governor of New York had chosen formality, writing "Hugh L. Carey" as if he were signing a bill into law. Because President John F. Kennedy had been assassinated five years before

Neary's opened its heavy wooden double doors, his portrait bore no inscription. But another Irish American President had written: "To Jimmy, A soul as forever green as the Auld Sod, Ron Reagan."

As the waitress withdrew and Neary hurried away to greet new customers, Goldstein turned to Leibholz. "What is the status of the search for Clements?"

"He's either lying low or long gone. None of our informants have seen him around his old haunts."

"Nobody's reported seeing any of the stolen goods floating around, either," Reiter added, reaching for a roll.

"What's your gut feeling, Al?" Bogdanovic asked.

"I think he'll surface sooner or later, maybe this weekend."

"My bet," Reiter said, chewing, "is that he's already found himself a new sugar daddy. The problem if he has is that the new man in his life is probably well heeled enough to have a summer retreat. If so, he could be beating the heat in the Hamptons or at some other gay resort."

"Fire Island," Flynn exclaimed. "God, how could I not have suggested that you look for Clements on Fire Island? In my first conversation with Griffith he mentioned Dodge had a house there. I'm sorry. I should have remembered before this."

"Al, Red, head out there as soon as we're finished lunch," Goldstein said.

The detectives exchanged eager looks.

"Okay. Forget the food," Goldstein said. "On your way out tell Neary it'll be only the three of us."

"It's a long shot, I know," Flynn said with a shrug as the detectives rushed out.

"But it's long shots that pay off the biggest," Goldstein replied. "And how could the detective story have survived this long without them? Not to mention the burst of inspiration, the slip of the tongue, the subtle giveaway that registered only in Hercule Poirot's little gray cells! And how could justice have been served were it not for a little old lady from St. Mary Meade recalling a quaint anecdote out of her busybody past that happens to be a parallel that unravels the mystery?"

Bogdanovic grunted. "Detective stories. The normal recreation of noble minds. Phooey."

"Ignore this Neanderthal, Arlene," Goldstein said. "Not to embarrass you, but I have to tell you that your work on this case has been really impressive. You are truly a first-class homicide detective."

Blushing, Flynn muttered, "That's very kind of you."

"So what the hell are you doing out in the boondocks? How many murder cases do you handle in a year that are in any way challenging? I mean real brain teasers."

"Last year, two."

"We get that many in a week. It's not my place to tell you how to run your career, but you belong where you can constantly test yourself. You belong in New York."

She gasped. "Chief, you're offering me a job?"

Goldstein elbowed Bogdanovic's ribs. "Johnny, this woman is *smart.*"

"It's a very flattering offer, Chief," she said, "but right now I'd prefer to concentrate on this case."

"I didn't expect an answer at this minute. All I hoped for was that you wouldn't reject the idea out of hand. Solve these murders and then take as much time as you want to chew it over."

Neary approached the table. "Excuse me, Chief. Telephone."

Watching Goldstein taking the call at the end of the bar, Bogdanovic said, "He's very high on you. Rightly so. He's offering you a great future."

"Johnny, please, let's keep our minds on this case."

"Very well. In mulling over the theory you laid out in the Chief's office, I've found a flaw. It involves Dodge's cape and the sword stick."

"What about them?"

"In your theory, Dodge met Valentine at the house and left the cape and the stick behind."

"Correct."

"If he did leave it at the house, that sword stick could not have been the murder weapon."

"Oh, Johnny Bogdanovic, you son of gun." Flynn sighed. "You just ruined a wonderful piece of deduction *and* our lunch."

Goldstein suddenly loomed beside her. "You can forget about

eating. And Leibholz and Reiter can forget going to Fire Island. Jimmy Clements has been located down in the Village. Al was right about him surfacing. Harbor Patrol found his body floating under a West Street pier."

33

Marked for Murder

SUNLIGHT REFLECTED OFF the gray river as if the Hudson were a mirror. Shimmering mid-afternoon heat brought out a piquant odor of kreosote in the wood planking and pilings of the old jutting wharf. The yellow tape marked "CRIME SCENE DO NOT CROSS" fluttering a little on a slight breeze wafting off the water lent the place a vague touch of carnival. Clustered behind it, shirtless men who had been sunbathing before the police came to order them away watched with a quiet that Flynn supposed could have stemmed from either respect for the dead or ghoulish fascination. Or the fearful realization that any one of them might have become the center of attention for a knot of police officers on a sultry May day in New York.

"Based on my fifteen years of pulling corpses out of this river," said Detective Sergeant M. C. Ludlum of Manhattan South Homicide, looking down at the covered body, "I'd say you can put him in the water sometime last weekend."

As he drew a yellow plastic sheet down from Jimmy Clement's head, Flynn thought that even in death the sandy-haired youth resembled cherubs in illustrated parochial school Bible stories. The only difference was a silver dollar–sized bruise on the right cheek and a gaping, blackened gash in the neck stretching from below the left ear to under the right.

"How did you I.D. him?" Bogdanovic asked.

"When the squad that pulled him out looked at his driver's license, they remembered his name on the alert you sent out."

"Is there any way of knowing if this is where he went in?"

"Not without a witness. But it's more than possible this was the spot. These piers crawl at night with guys out for sex, and there are gay bars all around the vicinity. It's a cruising area. That makes them easy prey for vultures looking for money. But we found fifty dollars in tens in his wallet and eight ones in his shirt pocket. Since that seems to rule out robbery, he could have run into somebody, or a gang, out for a night's gay bashing. With the warm weather, there's a whole lot of that going on."

"Does bashing include cutting throats?" Flynn asked.

"It's usually blunt trauma."

"What's your opinion on the kind of knife that was used? Big or small blade?"

Ludlum gazed down, thought a moment, and looked up at Bogdanovic. "John, you were in the Marines. Would you say that cut was made with a blade about the size of a bayonet?"

"It certainly took a large blade. Maybe a hunting knife."

"There's a bruise on his face," Flynn said.

"It's possible he got that going in," Ludlum replied. "Hit a piling, maybe. As to where he splashed, it could have been a long way up from here. The current could have carried him downstream. It's also possible he was killed somewhere else and dumped here. If it weren't for the body getting snagged by a piece of board that juts out just below the surface, he could have drifted all the way out to the Narrows or farther. If he had, I'd have one less case to clear."

"Consider this one mine," Bogdanovic said.

"You're welcome to it," Ludlum said, covering the face.

"If anything changes, I'll be back in touch," Bogdanovic said, walking away.

Flynn fell into step beside him but said nothing until they had passed the onlookers. "What odds are you giving that this has nothing to do with our murders? He just happened to be cruising and ran into a gay basher! From one to ten, where would that rank on the Bogdanovic coincidence meter?"

"You know where I stand on that."

"If whoever killed him did Dodge and Somerfield and tried to kill Griffith, you have to give him credit for variety of method. We've had one killed by a sword shoved into his brain, a gunshot aimed at another, one throat cut with a little knife and another with a big one. If you hadn't sent out an alert on Clements, there would be very little likelihood that Ludlum or anyone else could ever have connected a body from the river with the homicides of a couple of mystery writers. If you and I didn't know the Dodge and Somerfield killings were related, there would be nothing to lead *us* to believe they were committed by the same person. The methods were so different."

Bogdanovic stopped and abruptly turned. "Speaking of coincidences, at the Edgars dinner I was asked how I would go about murdering someone without being caught."

"The perfect murder! What did you suggest?"

"I said I'd lose the murder I wanted to achieve by hiding it among a series of randomly chosen strangers, each of the murders committed differently. Everyone found it amusing. But what if one of them had a reason to kill one of his colleagues and decided to give my scheme a try? Hell, any of those loonies might even have decided to do it for nothing more than an intellectual exercise. A little game of 'catch me if you can!' "

"Johnny, that is very, very scary."

"Here's something scarier. What if Dodge was not the one the killer really wanted dead? Suppose he was following my plan for a perfect murder, but that instead of the decoy victims being picked at random, he chose people he knows. What if it were Somerfield he had marked for murder? Or Griffith? We could be concentrating on the wrong victim. Spies! We've been looking for a complicated solution when a much simpler one was staring us in our faces. It had to be that someone at that dinner did it, using my plan for the perfect murder."

PART SEVEN

A Trout in the Milk

Some circumstantial evidence is very strong, as when you find a trout in the milk.

—HENRY DAVID THOREAU

Circumstantial evidence is occasionally very convincing, as when you find a trout in the milk, to quote Thoreau's example.

—SHERLOCK HOLMES

34

Process of Deduction

"LET US APPLY TO THIS CASE Sherlock Holmes's primary rule of the Science of Deduction," said the chief of detectives. "I say 'primary' because he enunciated it in one form or another in *The Sign of Four*, *The Beryl Coronet*, *Bruce-Partington Plans*, and *The Blanched Soldier*. He told Dr. Watson, 'When you have eliminated the impossible, whatever remains, however improbable, must be the truth.' That there is no connection between the murders of Dodge, Somerfield, and Clements and the shot taken at Griffith must fall, I believe, into the category of the impossible. Therefore, let's examine what's left. To do so we must begin with the murder of Jonathan Dodge, because it was first. Arlene, what do we know? No conjecturing, no theories. As Sergeant Joe Friday used to say on *Dragnet*, just give us the facts, ma'am."

"The body was discovered on Sunday morning in the boathouse at Traitor's Lair, recently bought by Morgan Griffith, a mystery writer. They were longtime friends, former journalists, both in their fifties. They had attended the Edgar Awards dinner of the Mystery Writers of America on Friday night where they engaged in a repartee that might be interpreted as the jesting of old pals or quite the contrary. The next time Griffith saw Dodge was in the boathouse. Dead. He had no explanation for Dodge being on his property.

"The cause of Dodge's death was a deep wound to the brain by an unknown weapon thrust through the mouth," Flynn went on. "The autopsy indicated that death occurred elsewhere and that the body had been roughly handled after death. Fibers found on Dodge's tuxedo suggest the body had been wrapped in multicolored fabric. The tux was dry, a significant fact inasmuch as there had been heavy rain on Friday night and Saturday. That he was still in a tuxedo is persuasive evidence that he had been killed Friday night or early on Saturday morning. His cape and a walking stick that had been in his possession at the dinner were found at his house in Gramercy Park. This indicates that he returned to his home after the dinner. We've found no evidence that he was murdered in the house."

She shot an impatient look at Bogdanovic.

"We're still waiting for the report from the forensics lab," she continued, "including results of the examination of Dodge's walking stick, which is a sword, to determine if it had been the murder weapon. In considering a motive, we have determined that among his circle of friends and professional associates there are plenty who had one. Shall I run down the list?"

"Please. But now I'd like the benefit of your thinking. And yours, too, John-Boy."

"Do you want them in any particular order?" Flynn asked.

"Any way you prefer."

"The obvious immediate suspect was Griffith. I interviewed him Sunday shortly after the body was discovered. That's how I learned that you and Johnny had been guests at the dinner. From the beginning he has been eager to provide whatever information he could to assist in the investigation. That made me and my boss a little nervous. But further reflection and events, such as his revelation that Dodge's Maltese Falcon cane was a sword stick that might have been the murder weapon, and the attempt that was made on his own life, led me to discount him as a suspect."

"And it was through Griffith," Bogdanovic interjected, "that Arlene and I learned of the existence of Gene Valentine, who then emerged as our prime suspect."

"Let's leave Valentine till last," Goldstein said. "Tell me about the suspects you had in your mind before you learned of the existence of Valentine."

"Because of Dodge's behavior at the dinner, it seemed logical in considering suspects to focus on guests who had intimate contact with him that night," Flynn went on. "You and Johnny were there and observed Dodge's demeanor, so I need not elucidate. Unless we choose to admit the possibility of accomplices in this crime, I have never seriously considered Eveland and Tinney. Plus the fact of their ages and frail physical conditions."

"They might have had help from a big man," Bogdanovic said.

Goldstein's eyebrows danced. "My old friend Wiggins?"

"Despite having a possible motive in Dodge's threats to expose him as a man operating with an alias," Flynn said, "Wiggins happens to be the only individual at that dinner, except you and Johnny, with an ironclad alibi. All his time is accounted for by several people."

"What about the artist?"

"Vernon Ney has motive—money and reputation—and possibly the means—a matador's sword. Opportunity? Insufficient data. He remains on the suspect list."

"How about the publisher?"

"Oscar Pendleton had the opportunity and no alibi. He also has motive. One may assume that in his role as a mystery store owner and mystery book publisher he is familiar with the weapons of murder and able to obtain them."

"When we called on him to talk to him, he was in the company of Myron Frank, Dodge's ex-agent," Bogdanovic said. "Frank also had motive and opportunity. If he and Pendleton were conspirators, he'd have means."

"I'm not big on conspiracies," Flynn said.

"Could either have done it alone?" Goldstein asked.

"Yes."

"Or helped one or both of the little old ladies?"

Flynn nodded.

"And what of the invisible man? The magician."

"Unless Jack Bohannon is playing tricks," she said, "I do believe he got caught in the rain as he claims. And where's the motive? A plausible one. Not a pipe dream about a TV show."

"Is that all the suspects?"

"Except Valentine."

"We're still deferring him. I can see why Dodge might be the object of a murder. Now tell me how his being killed relates to the demises of Somerfield and the kid. *Excluding* the possibility that everyone at Table Two was following the Bogdanovic formula for the perfect crime. Start with Clements."

"I think he could have been eliminated because he witnessed the murder of Dodge."

"But he was alive at noon the day after. If Dodge's killer knew the kid was a witness, how come the time lag between the murders?"

"This is supposition. The killer did not find out Clements was a witness till the kid told him so."

"Ah! The dread demon blackmail!"

"An alternative explanation," said Bogdanovic as he slouched in his chair, "is that the kid was an accomplice."

"Pray tell why he would assist in killing the golden goose."

"The flames of love were dying out?"

Goldstein shrugged. "Turn now to Alexander Somerfield."

"Because Dodge had a long relationship with Somerfield, he seemed a very hot possibility as Dodge's murderer," Flynn said. "As a former spy he would have had the means. He had opportunity. No one knows where he went after the party at the Usual Suspects. He owned a boat. He could have lured Dodge aboard *Karla,* killed him, and sailed up the river to dump him in Griffith's boathouse. And he could have enticed Clements to the boat, as well, killed him, and tossed him overboard as he sailed downriver on Saturday."

"But all that conjecturing went down the drain when he was also murdered," Bogdanovic muttered.

"Could he have been a witness to Dodge's murder? Or was he an accomplice who had to be gotten rid of? Why was he killed?"

"That was the beauty of Valentine," she said. "Somerfield's murder made sense in terms of the dark horse entry in our crowded field. The elusive, enigmatic Gene Valentine."

"That was based on the theory that the Somerfield manuscript is all about spies and that Dodge was at work on a similar book, but nonfiction, and that Gene Valentine figured in both? That he somehow found out about them and came to New York to dissuade the authors from publishing them? When he couldn't do that, he killed them?"

Flynn nodded. "Something like that."

"Evidence?"

"Not a shred."

"Put it to rest by finding Valentine. How do you do that?"

"Griffith told me he saw him a couple of weeks ago in the arrivals area of British Airways at Kennedy Airport," Flynn said. "Immigration and Customs should have a record of his flight and that will give us a passport number. And that could lead us to an address. Johnny has contacts among the cloak-and-dagger boys who may be helpful, as well."

Goldstein's eyes took on a distant look. "What was the line in *Tinker, Tailor, Soldier, Spy* that Ricky Tarr said? 'I've got a story to tell. It's all about spies.' "

"I believe that was in the TV version," Flynn answered. "But not in the novel."

Squirming in his deep chair and letting out a low groan as if he were in pain, Bogdanovic said, "If this is going to turn into a literary tea, count me out. If you need me, I'll be home." Pausing at the door, he said, "About Somerfield's book. Maybe it has someone else in it who'd rather not have the honor."

"Any suggestions?" Flynn asked.

He shrugged. "How about an old lover who found in my perfect murder plan a way to avenge a broken heart?"

35

Flashbacks

FOUR FLIGHTS UP at the top of a nineteenth-century mansion that the economics of twentieth-century real estate dictated be subdivided, the two-bedroom apartment with a skylight in the living room had been his for seven years, rented in anticipation of marriage. Had the woman not been wiser than he by calling it off, he recognized in retrospect, the union would have quickly foundered on the shoals of demands of conflicting careers. Like him, she married a job. Like him, she did not marry anyone else. Yet whenever he opened the door of his too-large-for-one apartment, he never failed to think of her fondly.

Slumping into a couch, he stared across the almost unfurnished living room that a woman's eye for decor might have graced with who knows what. His gaze fell on the only bookcase. Its four shelves had been filled not with thrillers that could lull a Harvey Goldstein to sleep or keep him up all night turning the pages, but textbooks. Charles Balleisen's *Principles of Firearms*. Herbert Block's *Crime in America*. In a yellow dust cover, *Criminal Investigation* by Swanson, Chamelin, and Territo. Paul Weston's *Police Organization and Management*. Binders filled with monthly editions of *The FBI Law Enforcement Bulletin*. A book by three FBI experts on serial killers— Robert K. Ressler, John E. Douglas, and Ann W. Burgess—*Sexual Homicide,* standing side by side with the *Encyclopedia of Forensic Science* by Brian Lane, ranging from acid to voice analyzers and voice prints. Kessler and Weston's *The Detection of Murder*. A black and gold looseleaf binder containing "Penal Law and Criminal Procedure Law of the State of New York." Two full shelves held NYPD training manuals and regulations. An inch-thick, pink-covered City of New York Police Department *Investigators' Guide* spanned everything from "Crime Scene" to "Testifying in Court." All that a homicide detective needed to know in order to carry out his job lay within easy reach.

"You've got all the technical stuff," Goldstein had said during a visit to the apartment shortly after he had selected Bogdanovic to become his assistant.

"But," he went on, his tone taking an admonishing quality, "I do not see one Sherlock Holmes or Hercule Poirot. Your library is long on the science of detective work, my boy, but where is the art?"

The next day Goldstein had returned from lunch carrying a thick book with a chocolate brown cover, *The Complete Sherlock Holmes*. As it dropped heavily onto Bogdanovic's desk, Goldstein said, "One should always begin a life of reading mystery novels with the Canon."

"You make it sound like a religion."

"Oh, it is, John-Boy," Goldstein answered as he disappeared into his office. "Sherlock Holmes is god of a very high church."

Later, placing the book in his lap, Bogdanovic had opened it in the middle and flipped pages, working toward the front, scanning the top lines of long pages dense with print:

"We were fortunate enough to catch an early train. . . ."

" . . . but there were footprints to prove the intrusion was an undoubted fact."

"We passed the pretty cottage where the murdered man had lived. . . ."

"Is there any point to which you would wish to draw my attention?"

"To the curious incident of the dog in the night-time."

"The dog did nothing in the night-time."

"That was the curious incident."

Stretching out on the couch, he opened the book again, selecting from the table of contents of *The Adventures of Sherlock Holmes* the title that seemed the most interesting, a fifteen-page story, "The Adventure of the Engineer's Thumb."

The next morning as Goldstein entered the car for the drive to One Police Plaza, Bogdanovic had greeted the chief of detectives with a riveting look. "So your famous detective wasn't so great after all. That gang of counterfeiters got clean away from him."

Goldstein looked at him blankly. "What the devil are you talking about?"

" 'The Engineer's Thumb.' The gang gave Sherlock the slip."

"Leave it to you," Goldstein had laughed, "to pick one of the few times the Sleuth of Baker Street did not collar the culprit. In that case, culprits. A grand tale, though. Now may I suggest you start at the beginning of that book? You must not judge Holmes by a single story."

Reading Dr. Watson's analysis of his newly found roommate in the second chapter of *A Study in Scarlet* had given Bogdanovic the idea to draw up a similar list of the pluses and minuses of Chief of Detectives Harvey Goldstein. Although the analysis provided many similarities to Holmes, it also contained numerous differences. But he had found in "The Final Problem" a summation of Dr. Watson's criminological tutor and friend which Sergeant John Bogdanovic would not hesitate to apply to Chief of Detectives Goldstein: "the best and wisest man whom I have ever known."

Goldstein's implorings, even haranguings, on the subject of the necessity of reading detective stories notwithstanding, *The Complete Sherlock Holmes* remained the only fictional work in a bookcase crammed with real crimes. But years after he had been given the book, barely a third of the good doctor's accounts of Holmes's adventures had been read.

In those years true crime had had a way of overwhelming and trivializing the fictional. Bogdanovic found that in real life dogs did not *not* bark in the nighttime. Observing sleeves and calluses of hands and fingers did not solve crimes. The ash of a cigarette had led to no unmasking of murderers. Amusing as it had been to read of Holmes's "Science of Deduction," it had little to do with the stark reality of murder in the modern world.

More than deductive reasoning would be needed to put the man who had murdered Jonathan Dodge, Alexander Somerfield, and Jimmy Clements in prison. It would be evidence, painstakingly gathered and analyzed in the crime labs. Bits and pieces. That's what made a murder case. In leading such an enterprise, he thought now on his way to the bedroom, there was no one better qualified than Arlene Flynn of the Stone County D.A. squad. Perhaps, soon, of the NYPD.

Unable to sleep, Bogdanovic went over the murders again and again until, at three in the morning, his mind settled on the Somerfield manuscript and the obstinate woman who refused to turn it over. With a grunt, he remembered Wiggins's name for Elvira Eveland, "Our Lady of the Mysteries."

A memory flashed back of a figure hesitating in the entrance to the Sheraton ballroom, a figure in black and white, like an old photograph. Chuckling, he recalled her flirting with him, her green eyes twinkling up at him like a schoolgirl's. He could still recall every word of their exchange:

"My, what a long drink of water you are, Sergeant. I happen to adore tall guys. When they're also dark and handsome, so much the better. Is that a gun under your coat? I hope so. There are so many at this shindig who need a slug of lead. Or two. Or six. Be a darling and fetch me a drink. Scotch, please. Neat. . . . Is our little affair to become like Rick's place in Casablanca? *Will there be an arrest here tonight? Am I the lucky dog?"*

At that moment Jonathan Dodge had stepped to her side and dragged her away. Returning, she had appeared shaken. But when she placed a hand on his shoulder, she had adopted a motherly tone. *"Be the darling smart young man I'm sure you are and tell us how you might go about ridding the world of a pest like Jonathan Dodge. So that you'd never be found out."*

After hearing his scheme for a perfect murder she planted a kiss on his cheek.

"My dearest Sergeant, that is positively scrumptious. You and I must have a lunch one day so that I may explore that devious brain of yours at leisure."

36

Science Report

AT TEN IN THE MORNING, when Arlene Flynn strode down a long corridor leading from a bank of elevators to Detective Sergeant John Bogdanovic's office in an unlovable brick pile known as One Police Plaza, she had a feeling of being watched. This sense of scrutiny began immediately upon stepping from the elevator. She confronted a photograph of Theodore Roosevelt taken by Jacob Riis in 1895. A reporter for the *Sun* newspaper and Roosevelt's close friend, Riis had previously used a camera to document appalling social conditions in New York immediately preceding Roosevelt's brief service as police commissioner. In passionate devotion to the police department and in upholding its professionalism, Bogdanovic had lectured her, no commissioner or member of the force before Teddy or since had been more zealous. "Except Chief Goldstein, of course," he added, proudly.

Turning from the elevators into the hallway toward Bogdanovic's office, she passed before the appraising eyes of his stolid and purposeful antecedents in the ranks of detectives, beginning with an 1880s heliotype of Chief of Detectives Thomas Byrnes. A walrus-mustached Irishman, he had commanded so much fear among denizens of the underworld that a simple "request" to a thief usually resulted in the prompt return of the purloined property. Having promised a newspaperman, Lincoln Steffens, that Steffens's lifted wallet would be returned "by Monday," Byrnes presented it on that date. "The detective's trade," he explained to the amazed writer, "consists not only in pursuing but in forming friendships with criminals."

Next to Byrnes on the wall hung a photograph of Alexander

Williams. A two-fisted but venal nineteenth-century detective nick-named "Clubber," he had coined an axiom that would be taught thereafter in law schools across the country. "There is more law in the end of a policeman's nightstick," Clubber had declared, "than in a decision of the Supreme Court."

Both Byrnes and Williams had been driven from the ranks of the force during a Roosevelt campaign to rid the department of corruption, forever, it seemed, the bane of the New York Police Department. Official misdeeds had also stained another of the stalwart sleuths on the wall, "Broadway" Johnny Broderick. So fearless a cop that he once dumped gangster Legs Diamond head first into a trash can, Broderick had seen his illustrious years as a detective end under a cloud amid accusations that he maintained a questionable association with hoodlum Owney Madden.

Photo after photo represented decade after decade of superior crime detection, from the bomb squad sleuths who tracked down the "Mad Bomber" George Metesky in the 1950s to those who put an end to the maraudings of the Son of Sam two decades later, side by side with others whose hard work and brains had solved less spectacular cases.

Did she want to enlist in these legendary ranks?

The last picture as she pushed open Bogdanovic's door was of Lewis Valentine, an honest cop plucked out of obscurity by Mayor Fiorello LaGuardia to be police commissioner for nearly all of La-Guardia's twelve years at City Hall. It had been Valentine who chastised a group of detectives because a gangster suspected of shooting a cop had stood in a police lineup without so much as a spot of blood on his Chesterfield overcoat. "When you bring in these bums, muss 'em up," he advised. "I want to see a spot or two of their blood on their fancy collars."

When the murderer of Dodge, Somerfield, and Clements was brought in, she thought, the killer would not have to worry about meeting a Clubber, a latter-day Broadway Johnny, or one of Lewis Valentine's muscular detectives. The murderer's rights would be scrupulously protected by the descendants of all the old cops on the walls, including Johnny Bogdanovic.

His office was him. Neat, orderly, and efficiently organized, the square room had a straight-from-the-NYPD-warehouse metal-sided desk with spotless Formica top, a pair of no-nonsense armless chairs covered in lime green stain-resistant coarse upholstery, a phalanx of black steel filing cabinets along an unadorned wall, and opposite them, a computer work station with flanking steel shelving stuffed with software packages and instruction manuals.

Surprisingly, he was not in.

Goldstein was. Coatless, with white shirtsleeves rolled up and teasing a long strand of wilted-looking hair, he resembled an unmade bed. He peered up, smiling. "Good morning, Arlene. Johnny called to say he'll be in late. He's got a lunch date."

"Does he? Did he say with whom?"

"Nope. But this should keep you busy till he's back." He handed her a slender manila folder. "It's the forensics report you've been waiting for."

Taking it and flipping back the cover, she said, "Have you studied it?"

"It's your case. The solution could be staring me in the face and I wouldn't recognize it."

"Let's just hope and pray it's here," Flynn said, clutching the folder to her chest and leaving the office. "We sure could use a break."

Entering an office as spartan as Bogdanovic's, she tossed her heavy shoulder bag onto a scarred yellow oak desk, sat in a dark wooden swivel armchair that might have been around in Roosevelt's day, and opened the report. Scanning the first three and a third pages, she learned that no evidence had been discovered to show that anyone had been murdered in Dodge's house.

A page of serological analysis cited numerous semen stains on bed sheets and in the master bathroom, but no bloodstains.

Microscopic examination of fibers from draperies, towels, sheets, blankets, two bathrobes, and carpeting in all the rooms proved unmatchable with the many colored fibers found on Dodge's tuxedo and the soles and heels of his black patent leather shoes. The paragraph concluded: "Further analysis pending."

The opera cape provided nothing in the way of clues.

Turning to the last page, she came to the analysis of the Maltese Falcon walking stick and with a sinking feeling in her stomach read the first two words: "Nothing remarkable. . . ."

37

Points of View

"NOTHING REMARKABLE in the microscopic serology study. No blood. No brain tissue," Flynn said dejectedly. "Not even a drop of sweat. The foil was as clean as a whistle. Fingerprint lab's analysis found only a gray smudge and the impression of a thumb and forefinger on the handle. Dodge's."

"The blade could have been washed clean," Goldstein said.

"What's washed is this case. Washed up." With a rueful expression she added, "And I am a washout."

Goldstein's face reddened. "That's nonsense, Arlene. You and John are making terrific progress."

She stood by his window. "I was positive we had the murder scene pinpointed. And the weapon," she said, watching a sailboat scudding up the East River. "I felt it in my guts." Glancing at the chair usually occupied by Bogdanovic, she sighed. "Well, so much for intuition."

Goldstein smiled, "I'm pleased to note that you did not say *feminine* intuition."

"It's been my experience, Chief," she said, striding to the door, "that intuition, like failure, is gender-neutral."

Yet as she returned to her office, she felt the trailing eyes of legendary masculine sleuths on the walls and thought they suddenly looked utterly disdainful. Closing the door on them, she welcomed the quiet. But a moment later it shattered with the ringing of her telephone.

"I know you're feeling blue at the moment," declared Goldstein flatly. "But I cannot let you think you've failed. I can say this to you now because Johnny's not around to roll his eyes and scoff at me. But there's a quote from good old Sherlock that I think you should mull over. It goes like this, more or less. Circumstantial evidence can be tricky. It may seem to point straight to one conclusion. But if you shift your point of view a little bit, you may discover that it's pointing to something completely different. So there it is. For whatever it's worth."

"Thanks, Chief. You're a sweet man."

"Don't let that get out. It'll ruin my reputation for crustiness. Now, take a deep breath or an aspirin and start going over everything once more. And when John gets back from lunch, the two of you review it together. I'm sure the answer's there."

Over the next two hours she found herself again in the mud at the steps to the boathouse. Inside, crouching beside a tidy corpse. Talking with Morgan Griffith as he smoked a cantankerous pipe that would not stay lit. In the library with its Chesterfield couch, green wingback chair, and costly carpet before a welcoming fire that might have cheered her had it not been for the body nearby. Touring the big empty house which had been so scary to her as a girl. Riveted by Griffith's recounting of the Edgar Awards dinner, and his portrait of Jonathan Dodge, a commanding figure at once so fascinating and repellent that she regretted never having known him, except through his books.

One by one before her mind's eye paraded all the colorful characters she had encountered, liked, and suspected: Wiggins, Ney, Pendleton, Frank, Bohannon, Tinney, and Eveland. Two she had not been allowed to know, Somerfield and Clements, because of a murderer. And one she hungered to meet, the mystery man with a past that seemed as romantic as his name. Elusive Gene Valentine.

Motives? Anger. Envy. Money. Reputation. Dashed hopes. Hurt feelings. Humiliation. All the human failings that had led one person to slay another since Cain and Abel.

Curiously, love had not figured into it. *Or had it?*

The evidence: A rainy night that left behind a corpse in a dry tuxedo and shoes with no mud on them. Mystifying fibers. A cape. A walking stick with a silver Maltese Falcon on the top and a long, thin sword lurking within. But no blood or brain tissue on it. One throat slit with a short plastic knife; another cut by what could have been a bayonet. A shot in the dark. A mysterious weekend boat ride. A rare book for sale. An airplane ticket for a journey to London and no one knew where after that. A manuscript Elvira Eveland had not allowed them to read.

The door opened and through it barged Bogdanovic, beaming as he strode to her desk. In one hand he held a small envelope. The other carried a bulky rectangular bundle wrapped in brown paper.

"Where've you been?" she demanded.

He sat on the corner of her desk. "During the now infamous Edgars Awards dinner, Elvira Eveland asked me to lunch with her someday. Today I took her up on it. We went to the Algonquin, the scene of the famous Round Table luncheons featuring Miss Dorothy Parker, Alexander Woollcott, and other celebrated wits of the Jazz Age. You see, I'm not the total literary ignoramus you and the Chief think I am. Elvira gave me this." He brandished the envelope. "It's a computer disk. Somerfield wrote on a computer."

He dropped the package. It hit the desk with a thud.

"And that is a print-out. I shall go through the disc on my computer at home and you can cozy up with the manuscript when you go beddie-bye tonight."

"Tonight, hell! I'm going to start reading *now*. How did you get Elvira to part with the book?"

"You want a man's job done, send a man to do it."

Excitedly ripping the brown paper, she said, "This must be how Sam Spade felt when he finally got hands on that black bird."

The title page read:

Below the Line
a novel

by
Alexander Somerfield

PART EIGHT

Between the Lines

In every operation there is an above the line and a below the line. Above the line is what you do by the book. Below the line is how you do the job.

—JOHN LE CARRÉ, *A PERFECT SPY*

38

Page-Turner

As in all page-turners, the opening was a grabber:

"Something had to be done about Nguyen Lau. And right away. But who could handle it?"

The setting was Saigon in 1966. But Flynn soon found herself drawn back in time and into the company of a man called Malone.

Born during the Great Depression, he had come of age when Eisenhower was a president derided as "chairman of the bored," a reference to Malone's "silent generation" that would be derided by others as self-centered do-nothings. The first generation to grow up in the shadow of possible nuclear war, they had borne the duties and responsibilities required of them and planned their lives with the knowledge that their personal dreams might have to be interrupted, as Malone's hopes for a quick start on a career as a reporter after graduation from journalism school were put on hold by service in the Army.

Except for those years, he had carried a press pass for more than a decade, first in small towns learning his trade of chasing stories, then in bigger places with bigger stories, and at last, in the supreme news town of all: New York. His credentials had admitted him to the corridors of power of government and smoke-filled rooms of party politics, into lavish festivities in ballrooms of grand hotels, into cold-water tenements where murders had been committed, and anywhere else where he might find a story.

On a notepad she scribbled, "Which one is Malone? Is he Dodge? Somerfield? Griffith? Valentine?"

All were of Malone's age.

She resumed reading.

Malone had arrived at the Saigon Bureau on the sixth floor of the Caravelle Hotel four months after the Johnson landslide buried Barry Goldwater. His decision to ask for the assignment had stunned the normally unflappable Harry Putnam. "Jesus Christ All Mighty," he thundered. "Why Veet-naam?"

"The story's there, Harry. President Johnson had it right. During the campaign, he said, 'Vote for Goldwater and we'll be in a wider war in Vietnam.' Well, millions voted for Goldwater and, sure enough, we're in a widening war! The escalator is going up, Harry, and I need to be on it."

Putnam shifted his cigar from the right side of his mouth to the left, an unmistakable signal of disgust. "Know what I think, Malone? I think you've got a death wish."

A week later, Malone found himself en route, and the day after he checked in with Dave Bernstein, the bureau chief, he was up to his eyes in elephant grass and learning the vocabulary of his war. Grunts taught him that his meal of C-rations was beans and motherfuckers. Their lieutenant with his single brass insignia of rank was a butter bar. Beehive rounds were artillery shells that blew up and sprayed thousands of projectiles that were like nails with fins. Anyone who walked carelessly was a diddy-bopper who was begging to lose his legs to a V.C. land mine no bigger than a man's finger and, so, called a finger charge. A fragmentation grenade was a frag, and to off a gung-ho lieutenant was to frag a butter bar. The Long Range Reconnaissance mission he was on was a LURP. They had been transported by a chopper to a landing point (LZ) where the LURP was to start. If he didn't make it back, he would have experienced a No. 10: the worst. That day, two grunts who should have been at home dating co-eds came up No. 10. To the grunts, Malone was the FNG—fucking new guy.

Flynn glanced at her watch and realized she had been reading for almost an hour.

On the notepad she wrote: Was/Is Malone Valentine?

A few minutes later the pad received a new name.

"What's your poison, Hoover?" Malone asked as a Vietnamese waiter solicited their drink order.

"Scotch if they have it," Hoover replied.

Malone chuckled. "If they have it? Hell, in this cruddy war we have everything. Lyndon Johnson sends us all the comforts of home. Well, almost all." As the waiter left them, he whispered, "Ten to one that guy's a Viet Cong."

"As long as he comes back with scotch," Hoover said, "who cares what his politics is? Or should that be 'politics are'?"

"Let's drink to clarity," Malone said.

"Quite a view from up here," Hoover said, gazing out the window. "It reminds me of Paris. Saigon was a French colony, of course." In the far distance, yellow dots of light floated down in the black night. "Flares?" he asked, nodding at them.

"There's a good deal of night patrolling in the boonies," Malone said, watching the lights and thinking about fireflies flitting around his house when he was a boy. "If the wind is right and the windows were open, you could hear the shooting. But no one opens windows." The glass through which they peered was crisscrossed with wide strips of tape, giving the windows the appearance of diamond-shaped panes in English country houses. "The tape keeps glass from spraying the room," he said, "if a V.C. bomb should go off outside."

"Do they?"

"We're smack in the middle of town," Malone said. "That's the Opera House Square below. The Brink barracks is close. That's the main American officers' billet. Military headquarters isn't far from here. Plus the U.S. Embassy. The Continental Hotel, just opposite us, was fragged—sorry, bombed—a week ago. A V.C. kid buzzed by on a motorbike and lobbed a grenade through the window of the fairly good Italian restaurant on the ground floor. So you see, we're pretty much ground zero."

The waiter returned with the scotches and to present their menus. "This is weird," Hoover said, studying the bill of fare. "It seems a little obscene to be ordering French cuisine when you can look out the window and know that men are killing one another a few miles away. And for what?"

"Hearts and minds," Malone said, smiling.

She jotted: Hoover = Griffith!!
The next chapter presented yet another character.

Kershner introduced himself at a low-key reception at the American Embassy to welcome President Johnson's emissary, Maxwell Taylor. In Saigon on yet another mission, the retired general's task was to determine what Ambassador Henry Cabot Lodge and General William Westmoreland needed to turn Lyndon Johnson's policy in Vietnam into an unquestionable success.

"You're the new man in Dave Bernstein's shop," Kershner said. "We should have lunch. I'll call your office to arrange a convenient time."

Bernstein knew all about him. He had come to the CIA after excelling in Oriental studies at Yale. After he left New Haven he had served as an assistant to Senator Joseph R. McCarthy's chief aide, sallow-faced and vitriolic Roy Cohn, and counsel to the McCarthy Communist-baiting committee leader of the early 1950s, Robert Kennedy. Surviving McCarthy's downfall, he turned to journalism and somewhere along the way had been recruited—or volunteered—to help the Central Intelligence Agency in thwarting communism in Indochina. His arrival in Saigon had been noted in 1961, barely two weeks after the inauguration of Bobby's brother as President. His assignment was to recruit reporters who would then put a pro-Kennedy spin on their stories.

Flynn scrawled:

Kershner = *Somerfield!*
Hoover = Griffith
Malone = Valentine

Reading on, she joined Malone and Kershner for a meal.

The luncheon proved pleasant, a sumptuous Chinese banquet in the Cholon section of the city. Detecting no efforts to recruit him, Malone was nonetheless impressed that Kershner had learned a great deal about him.

"When you covered the Republican Convention in 1964, what did you think of Goldwater?" Kershner asked.

"Being a newsman," Malone answered, "I found the senator's views interesting. As a realist, I recognized that he didn't have a snowball's chance in hell of winning. Not against Johnson. Not when voters were still caught up in the sentiment that followed the assassination of Kennedy. That's why Nixon didn't try for the nomination. He knew that 1964 was going to be a Democrat year."

"Do you think Johnson will win in 1968?"

"Only if he wins this war."

"Do you think we can win it?"

"Of course."

"A lot of people think we don't belong in Vietnam."

"They're fools."

Lifting a teacup, Kershner smiled. "I'll drink to that."

Onto the notepad went: "Kershner (Somerfield) recruiting Malone (Valentine). For what?"

Looking up at the window, Flynn saw that darkness had fallen over the city, but her reading continued.

Crisply dressed in a suit tailormade in Hong Kong, Kershner greeted Malone at the bar of the Officers' Club. "The word is," he said, shaking his head ruefully, "that you nearly bought the farm by playing hero on your last trip out to the boondocks."

Malone looked at him suspiciously. "How do you know that?"

"When an ace reporter almost gets himself wasted in saving a grunt's life, word gets around fast. What are you drinking?"

"Scotch. Neat."

"Me, too," Kershner told the bartender. "There's another thing I like about you, Malone. You take your poison straight."

"What else do you like about me?"

Kershner lit a cigarette. "You're a patriot."

Malone lit a pipe. "Am I?"

"That's why you volunteered to come to Vietnam."

"Like Rick in *Casablanca*," Malone said, "I was misled. I thought Saigon was a health resort."

"Since there is no future in Vietnam and never has been for making a great reputation as a newsman, unless you're against the war, I had to wonder what the hell a smart guy like you was doing here. You seemed to me to belong back in the States, getting rich on your smarts. First I thought you were collecting material for a book. In a year or so, I figured, Malone would be on the best-seller list with the great novel about Vietnam, and a year after that Malone would be out in Hollywood as exec producer of the TV movie based on the book and screwing movie stars."

"I wish I'd thought of it. You should be an agent. Pardon the pun."

"As the Nazi said to Rick, we have a dossier on you."

"Why am I not surprised?"

"When I looked at it the first time, it was not at all what I expected. I figured you'd be one more left-wing bleeding heart reporter determined to make a name by exposing the quagmire that is our involvement in Vietnam. But you didn't go in for superstar stuff. Sometimes when I saw your reports among the samplings of coverage that Washington sends back to us, you looked like just another grunt."

"I try to fit in," Malone said dryly.

"Some people would say that nearly getting blown away in a daring life-saving rescue of a grunt by some snot-nosed V.C. kid with a grenade under his shirt is carrying 'fitting in' a little far. But your gallantry came as no surprise to me. I found your patriotic streak showing itself way back in 1956. You had a draft deferrment in college. But as soon as you graduated, you enlisted in the Army anyway."

"By then there was no Korean War. Ike had ended it. And from what I knew of Ike, he wasn't about to get us in another one."

"You enlisted because you believed it your patriotic duty."

"Look. What's all this about, Kershner?"

"How would you like to help speed the end of this war?"

"Do you want me to assassinate Ho Chi Minh? General Giap?"

"The man I have in mind uses the name Nguyen Lau."

Malone laughed. "What could wasting a Tu Do Street whoremonger possibly have to do with helping win the war?"

"People are not always what they say they are."

Looking up from the page, Flynn tugged her lip and muttered, "Tu Do Street."

Her watch showed eight o'clock. Deciding to finish reading at home, she stuffed the manuscript and notepad in her commodious bag. Passing Bogdanovic's office, she noted no light under the door and wondered when he had called it a day.

Waiting for an elevator under the watchful eyes of Theodore Roosevelt, she silently asked, "So where's Dodge in this book?"

39

Roman à Clef

THE PHONE WOKE her at seven. "I tried calling last night," said Benson, breezily. The quiet around him suggested he was not at home but in the office. "Your line was constantly busy."

"I had it off the hook. I was reading. Not for pleasure!"

"What if you were? You're entitled. How goes the case?"

She thought for a long moment. "We're getting there. I hope by tonight to tell you we're *nearly* there. I think Griffith can help speed us along the way."

Considering the clock, she wondered what hour authors got out of bed, then dialed Griffith's New York number. When he did not pick up and the answering machine came on, she hung up and tried Traitor's Lair.

He sounded wide awake. "This is a coincidence. I was going to phone you in an hour or so."

"For any particular reason?"

"I couldn't sleep. The damned birds kept me awake. I'm a very light sleeper. When I bought this place I never thought about how noisy birds can be. I'm curious about the case. I'm one of those terrible people who peek at the endings of detective stories. If there's anything I can do . . ."

"That's why the call. I've been reading Somerfield's book."

"Below the Line? Fantastic. How'd you get it?"

"It wasn't easy. I was hoping you could help me sort out the characters. For instance, I haven't got a clear picture as to who's who. Do you expect to be at Traitor's Lair all day?"

"Through the weekend, actually. A mover is bringing some of my things up from the city this morning. I thought items from my collections would make this place more like home. But most of the stuff will be books."

"Any of them by Dodge?"

"These are primarily novels. Which of his interests you?"

"Having read Somerfield's manuscript, I think it might be of help to me to have a look at Dodge's Vietnam memoir."

"Incident on Tu Do Street."

"Do you remember if Gene Valentine had been in Saigon at the time Dodge wrote about?"

"We all were there."

"Well, I don't want to pick over your memory on the phone. If it won't upset your moving plans, may Sergeant Bogdanovic and I drop in to see you today?"

"To blazes with the movers. Nothing's more urgent than your finding this killer."

"I'll phone ahead to alert you that we're on our way."

"As far as I'm concerned," he said, angrily, "the sooner the better."

"I'm calling Johnny Bogdanovic now to arrange it."

Bogdanovic answered on the fourth ring, groggily.

"You sound pretty awful," she said. "Up all night?"

"Reading you know what. I hope you made more sense out of it than I did. I thought people in a . . . what the hell do you call a book like that?"

"A *roman à clef.*"

"I thought people were supposed to be *thinly* disguised."

"The problem," Flynn said, "is that you and I don't know the real people well enough to say, 'Aha! That's Dodge.' He's Somerfield, although I'm pretty sure Somerfield is Kershner in the book. At any rate, I've been on the phone with Griffith and he's agreed to decipher for us. He's up at Traitor's Lair. How soon do you think you can pry yourself away from Hell on the Hudson and get yourself to God's country?"

"I was planning to touch base with Al and Red first thing to see if their search of the arrivals and departures records at JFK turned up Valentine."

"Excellent. Then, could you swing by Dodge's house and pick up a copy of *Incident on Tu Do Street* and bring it with you? Give me a call when you're about to leave for here. I'll be at my desk in Benson's office. He goes to court tomorrow on a case I should brief him on. And you would not believe what's backlogged on my desk since Sunday in the way of new cases. Crime may not pay, but that doesn't keep people from trying."

"Tell me about it!"

Hanging up the phone, Bogdanovic sat naked on the edge of his bed and looked out the window at pale gray sky portending another day of sweltering heat, foul smells, and short tempers that in all likelihood would spell violent deaths for several of the city's citizens by the same time tomorrow. And a few more, should the moon be full. But they would be spur-of-the-moment homicides. Detectives would look into glazed eyes in dazed faces and hear the same old story of too many people rubbing against each other in far too small a space. "I didn't mean it. He got on my nerves. I grabbed my gun." Or knife. A club. Or he had had it and did it to her. And more and more it was him or her and a baby that wouldn't stop crying or kept wetting its pants. Not to mention the drug killings. Few and far between came the cases where one human being sat down and coolly calculated and then carried out a murder of the kind that got routinely solved by a clever copper in a trenchcoat on TV.

At a few minutes after eight o'clock he found Leibholz and Reiter waiting in his office, dressed for the weather in short-sleeve shirts and summer-weight trousers, service pistols holstered on their belts. As usual, Leibholz began. "Only two people named Valentine passed through any of the airlines at Kennedy in the past month. Mildred W. Valentine of Jersey City, a retired school-teacher going to and from a visit to relatives in Ireland. And a Timothy Valentine, age seventy-two, the Bronx."

"Too old to be our Valentine."

"A computer check at the passport center in New England," said Reiter, "also came up empty regarding anyone with a monicker that was anything close to a Gene Valentine."

"What about the State Department's files in Washington?"

The detectives shook their heads.

"A Gene Valentin-o lives in Maryland," Leibholz said.

"But he's been in Italy for two months," Reiter added.

"Obviously, our Valentine used an alias," Leibholz said.

"That fits," Bogdanovic replied. "The guy's probably got a dozen bogus identities. The man is, or was, a spook."

"How about getting in touch with your contacts in the world of spookdom?" Leibholz asked.

"If you try to get them to open up about one of their own, which this Valentine appears to be," Bogdanovic replied, "those guys make a mockery of the police department's so-called blue wall of silence. It's like butting your head against the damn Berlin Wall."

"Any suggestions?" Reiter asked.

"Nothing at the moment. But hang loose, guys. Who knows what might turn up? This case has more twists and turns than a plate of spaghetti."

"Where do you go from here, John?" Leibholz asked.

"First, I pick up a book. Then I head for the sticks," he replied, heading to the door. "I just hope that Stone County is a lot cooler than this concrete and glass blast oven."

A freshening breeze stirred trees in Gramercy Park, but the interior of Dodge's unaired house felt stifling. Looking around, he found the work of Leibholz's crime scene team. Fingerprinting dust clouded the surface of tables, doorknobs, the wires and plugs of the missing electronic equipment, and the connectors which had hooked up Dodge's computer, presumed taken by Clements. Closet doors and drawers of tables, cabinets, and bureaus had been left wide open. Newspapers and magazines had been examined and dumped in disheveled piles. Expensive suits looked like heaps of rags earmarked for the homeless.

From bookshelves filled with Jonathan Dodge titles he took down two copies of *Incident on Tu Do Street* in a row of paperback editions. Wondering if they might differ from the original, he looked for hardcovers and found one copy.

Then, using a dusted telephone, he informed Flynn he was on his way to Stone County. Locking up the house, he imagined antique dealers descending upon its treasures once the estate had been probated and the furnishings put on auction. As he drove away, he wondered what would happen to his possessions in the event of his death and envisioned them in a flea market. An hour later he was parking in front of the imposing Victorian edifice housing Stone

County's courts and offices of District Attorney Aaron Benson. Using his car phone, he informed Arlene Flynn, "I'm out front."

Moments later she bounded down the steps with a large bag slung over her shoulder. Looking cool and comfortable in a beige blouse and brown slacks, she came round to the driver's side of the air-conditioned car. He rolled down the window and felt a rush of heat.

"Since I know the way, why don't I drive?" she said.

He slid to the passenger's side.

Taking the wheel, she said, "Did you find the book?"

"Two paperbacks and a hardcover."

"That's excellent," she said, stuffing the books in her bag. "We'll each have our own."

40

"Elementary, My Dear Watson!"

GRIFFITH GREETED THEM at the front door of Ilona Troy's old house in blue jeans and the faded denim shirt of Sunday, the pipe jutting from a corner of his mouth. Removing it, he shouted, "Hello!"

The smoking pipe went into a breast pocket of the shirt.

"Excuse me, but that's still lit," Flynn exclaimed.

"It's all right. I've only set myself on fire twice, never seriously. My entire wardrobe is riddled with burn holes. The movers have come and gone. And I've unpacked some of my kitchen things. May I get you each some coffee before we settle down to our day's work?"

"I'm hot enough as it is," Bogdanovic grumbled.

"And I've had my morning cuppa," Flynn said cheerily. "As the English would say."

Griffith stepped aside for them to enter the house. "I have cleared the library out somewhat. But no fireplace ablaze today, Miss Flynn. Sorry."

"Sunday was a little on the nippy side," she explained for Bogdanovic's benefit as they passed through the foyer with its sweeping curved staircase. "What about your window? Fixed?"

"Fulmer was here yesterday. But he says the hole in the wall is going to take a little longer to patch, I'm sorry to report."

Stepping into the room, she glanced around, taking in the Chesterfield couch, the wingback chair, carpet, the cold hearth, and the few remaining cartons. As her eyes reached the window, they found the desk and the computer's position unchanged.

"You may do as you like, Mr. Griffith," she scolded. "But if I were in your position, I'd feel awfully uncomfortable working near that window as long as Valentine remains at large."

Griffith looked aghast. "Surely you don't believe Gene is still in these parts?"

"If he targeted you once, I have no reason to assume he won't try again. At the very least if you are not going to move your desk, you ought to put up drapes."

Griffith stared at the desk. "I take your point. I'll move it as soon as we're through."

"When we talked in this room on Sunday," she said, settling in the wingback chair, "you said you'd like to be Dr. Watson to my Sherlock Holmes. I'm afraid I brushed you off. But now I believe you can be of inestimable help."

"That's great!"

"John and I have read Somerfield's manuscript and, frankly, it left us bewildered. I was hoping that with your grasp of writing techniques and your intimate knowledge of the people that his characters appear to have been based on, you'll be able to sift the wheat from the chaff, so to speak. Have you read the book?"

"Elvira had it under lock and key. I'm amazed that she let you have a copy."

Flynn smiled at Bogdanovic. "We have Johnny to thank."

Leaning against the mantel, he shrugged. "We would have gotten one eventually."

"Please have a seat on the couch, Sergeant," Griffith said.

"I don't mind standing."

Flynn opened her bag. "Before we get down to the books.—"

Griffith turned to her. "Books?"

She drew Dodge's volumes and the manuscript from her bag. "I thought we'd compare Somerfield's *Below the Line* with *Incident on Tu Do Street.*"

"Keep in mind one's fiction and the other nonfiction."

"But they do deal with the same subject."

"I presume, or you would not have brought them both. But I wouldn't know."

"Before we get started, I'd like Sergeant Bogdanovic to see the boathouse." She looked at her shoes, then up at Griffith. "I'd hate to ruin these. I wonder if I could impose on you, Mr. Griffith, to show it to him."

Bogdanovic looked puzzled. "Am I supposed to be looking for anything in particular?"

"I'd like your opinion, and Mr. Griffith's, on whether our idea about Dodge being brought up here on a boat makes sense from the vantage point of the condition of the boathouse."

Griffith's eyes widened. "A boat? Yes! Jonathan could have been brought up here on Somerfield's yacht."

"Can you hear boats passing on the river?"

"I haven't really noticed. I don't recall hearing any."

"Do you know if Valentine knew how to operate a boat?"

"I do remember him mentioning he'd been in the Navy."

"You served in the Army?"

"Correct. So did Alex and Jonathan."

Bogdanovic asked, "What branch were you in?"

"The Signal Corps. A lot of guys with journalism or communications training were put in the Signal Corps because somebody at the Pentagon assumed we could repair radios. All I know about them is how to turn them on."

"What branch was Dodge in?" Flynn asked.

"Jonathan served as an aide to some general. He prided himself on having pull."

"And Somerfield?"

"He served during World War II. Office of Strategic Services. The OSS was the grandfather of the CIA."

"Thanks. I know."

Bogdanovic moved to the door leading to the sloping lawn. "Ready for the grand tour when you are, Mr. Griffith."

Outside, Griffith whispered, "She is really something. What a brilliant mind."

"Arlene is tops, all right," Bogdanovic said, as they began the muddy downhill walk. "But I wish she'd told me I was going to be tramping around in the mud. I would have worn my boots. These shoes cost me two hundred bucks."

"I expect the idea just came to her. But this notion about Jonathan being brought up here on a boat is exciting. I've been puzzled about how the body got up here. The only way to reach the property is by the driveway. And I would have heard a car."

"If you were here."

"I was. I drove up directly after Wiggins's party."

"When did you arrive?"

"A little after two in the morning. Then I stayed up a while, cranking away at the old sausage machine."

"Beg pardon?"

"Agatha Christie said that when she wrote another Hercule Poirot or Jane Marple novel, she felt as if she were a sausage machine. Think of what the old girl might have ground out if she'd had word processing."

"I noticed that you use a computer."

"Yes. I reluctantly gave up my portable typewriter when my publisher started bugging me to hand in manuscripts on disc as well as paper. Apparently it saves a publisher money during the production process. What I discovered, happily, is that the new technology has made me a better writer. Knowing I don't have to retype pages when I make changes, I'm not loathe to edit myself."

They reached the boathouse. "I see why you decided to demolish it," Bogdanovic remarked.

"I can't help thinking," Griffith said morosely, "that if I'd put Fulmer to work sooner, Jonathan might still be alive."

"I doubt that very much," Bogdanovic said, going inside.

Griffith went no farther in than the doorway. "He was lying about where you're standing, Sergeant."

Bogdanovic peered through the dim interior to the opposite wall. "The jetty is over that way?"

"There's a sliding door. Please be careful of the flooring. There are lots of loose boards."

They creaked and popped as Bogdanovic crossed the dark room. Opening the door with an effort, he squinted from the glare of sunlight reflecting off the river. Walking to the end of the jetty, he found the weathered planking surprisingly solid underfoot and the supporting beams and pilings steady.

"What do you think, Sergeant?" Griffith shouted. "Could a boat have moored?"

"If she had a good skipper at the helm, easily."

Returning to the house, they found Flynn seated yoga-style on the carpet with her back resting against the wingback chair. Somerfield's manuscript lay in her lap, the hardcover edition of *Incident on Tu Do Street* atop it, and her hands folded upon them.

Griffith grinned boyishly. "You look like a Vietnamese Buddhist monk, except you have no begging bowl."

"I thought Buddhism was like the Catholic Church. No women allowed in the clergy."

He dropped onto the couch and fished the pipe from the shirt pocket. "Do you mind if I smoke, Sergeant B?"

"If it's okay with her," Bogdanovic said, sitting next to him, "it's fine with me."

"I know she doesn't object. Or, if she does, she's much too polite to say so."

"I like the aroma of pipe tobacco," Flynn said. "If I were ever to take up smoking, I'd go for pipes. They do suit you. My image of a man at work on a book has always included a pipe clenched in his teeth."

He tamped the black bowl with a fingertip and drew a box of Rosebud wooden matches from the shirt. "Please tell that to my dentist. He's always scolding me about the nicotine stains."

"And your manicurist?"

"Beg pardon?"

"You have a habit of poking a finger in the bowl and getting ashes on it and under the nail."

Griffith studied his blackened forefinger. "It gets burned a lot."

"Was Somerfield a pipe smoker?"

"The occasional postprandial cigar."

"What about Dodge?"

"He had a four-pack-a-day cigarette habit until his doctor told him to quit or die of a heart attack."

"That's interesting."

"It is?"

"The lab report on the Maltese Falcon sword stick made note of a gray smudge on the handle. I thought Dodge might have shared your habit of tamping a pipe with his fingertip."

"Now that I think about it, *Valentine* always smoked a pipe."

199

"Are you certain about that?"

"Quite. And pipe-smoking tends to be a lifetime thing."

"Odd. In the photo of you and him on the wall of your apartment you're holding a pipe, but he's got a cigarette."

"Perhaps he forgot his pipe that day."

"That's probably it. Do you know if he had a favorite brand of pipe tobacco?"

"Hardly! And if I did, what's it matter?"

She cracked a sly smile. "What a shocking statement from a student of the man who wrote the monograph on distinguishing the ashes of one hundred forty forms of cigar, cigarette, and pipe tobaccos."

Griffith grinned and twirled the pipe between his fingers.

" 'To the trained eye,' he told Dr. Watson, 'there is as much difference between the black ash of a Trichinopoly and the white fluff of bird's-eye as there is between a cabbage and a potato.' "

"You told me you favor Balkan Sobranie."

"You have a sharp memory, Miss Flynn."

"If I asked Sergeant Bogdanovic's lab people to examine that gray smudge on Dodge's Maltese Falcon walking stick to determine if it is pipe tobacco ash, what do you suppose they'd report?"

"If they could reach a conclusion, which I doubt, they might tell you that someone who smoked a pipe may have handled it."

"And what if the report found it was Balkan Sobranie ash?"

"Then you would be looking for a Balkan Sobranie smoker. How many are there in the world, I wonder?"

"The question would be, 'How many are there who knew Jonathan Dodge?' Even more significantly, how many Balkan Sobranie smokers at the Edgar Awards dinner would have known him well enough to be permitted to handle his most prized walking stick?"

"Anyone in the coat check room could have handled it."

"He didn't check it," Bogdanovic said. "He had it and the cape with him the whole time. He said he never checked the cane because he was certain it would be stolen."

"Excuse me, Miss Flynn, but all this strikes me as trivial."

She threw up her hands. "There you go again, forgetting your Holmes. His method was.–"

"Founded upon the observation of trifles."

"Trouser knees. Shirt cuffs. Boots. Boot laces. The sleeves, particularly elbows. Callosities. Finger—"

Stirring impatiently, Griffith muttered, "Yes, yes. Fingernails as well, as you've demonstrated."

"And the importance of fibers," she said, stroking the Oriental carpet beneath her. "It's exquisite. Somerfield certainly steered you right when you bought this Persian rug."

"It's not Persian. It's from Afghanistan."

"Ah, yes, you've been in Afghanistan."

"Cute, Miss Flynn. Bravo! As I observed once before, you've caught up on your Sherlock."

"The golden dragon suggests neither Persian nor Afghan. When I first saw it Sunday morning, I thought it looked Chinese. I understand that the way you tell the difference between carpets, and where they were made, is by the knotting."

"So I believe."

"That means you have to look at the back. Would you mind if I had a peek at the back of this one?"

A slow smile overspread his lips. "I have a sneaky feeling that while I was showing Sergeant B the boathouse, you did."

"May I show Sergeant B the caked mud on the back that I am positive will match any samples of earth that we might take from the lawn between here and the boathouse?"

"Is there any way I could prevent you?"

"You could demand a search warrant. That would take District Attorney Benson about an hour, at most."

"May I point out you had no warrant when you had your peek?"

"That's an excellent legalistic point that your lawyer may choose to pursue in the event you decide to brazen it out and not confess to the four murders."

Bogdanovic leapt to his feet. *"Four?"*

"Jonathan Dodge, Alexander Somerfield, Jimmy Clements, and a Vietnamese whose name in Somerfield's book is Nguyen Lau. Would you care to give us his real name, Mr. Griffith?"

"Tran Van Giap. As Dodge pointed out in *Incident on Tu Do Street,* he was no relation to the famed General Giap who led the

North Vietnamese to victory in that war."

He paused, puffing on the pipe and smiling at the same time.

"May I ask how you knew it was I? And, please, don't tell me it was elementary."

"I'll tell you the how," she said, "after you tell me the why."

41

Echo from the Woods

"IT BEGAN WHEN I heard that Alex was writing a *roman à clef* about our Vietnam days."

"If Somerfield was tight-lipped about his work, how did you hear about it?"

"Jonathan told me. He got it from Margaret Tinney, who got it directly from Elvira Eveland, of course. He came to me livid about it. He was furious that Alex would be rooting around in the same territory that Jonathan covered in *Incident on Tu Do Street*. Being Jonathan, he made up his mind to go back to Vietnam to see if he could locate the Saigon detective who had investigated the murder of Tran Van Giap. Jonathan expected to come back with the full story and get it into print before Alex's book came out. In my case, since I was the one who'd killed Giap, I didn't want either book published. However, I could have lived with Alex's, because it was a novel, whereas Jonathan was planning to do another True Crime blockbuster best-seller. When he said he was leaving the country the next day, and 'returning to the scene of the crime,' and then looked right at me and talked about people not being what they say they are, I realized I had to stop him. I whispered in his ear that I had gotten a disc of Alex's book."

"Had you?"

"Oh yes. I managed to make a copy of Alex's floppy disc a few days after he delivered it to Elvira. I plucked it off her desk right under her nose. Her office is always such a mess that she never missed it. Then I copied it into my own computer's hard drive and had the floppy back on Elvira's pile within two hours, while she was having one of her legendary Algonquin lunches."

"Jonathan grabbed the invitation to see Alex's book?"

"He was drooling in my apartment barely half an hour after he got the Grand Master award. I had gotten home a few minutes earlier. He was drunker than a sailor on a Saturday night toot and eventually passed out on my couch without even removing his opera cape. There he was, out like a light, his head tilted back, his mouth gaping, and the Maltese Falcon sword stick lying across his lap. That's when I realized that I couldn't permit him to go back to Vietnam. That the only way out of my dilemma was to kill him. Quickly, humanely, as little mess as possible. I did it and went to Wiggins's party."

"Then you came home to face the age-old dilemma."

"Yes. The problem that all murderers have. What to do with the *corpus*. Jonathan Dodge was not a small figure, as you know. I saw immediately that I would need help in getting him out of my apartment to wherever I was going to leave him. Fortunately, I was in the process of moving possessions to Traitor's Lair and had already enlisted the aid of my building superintendent on two occasions, along with his ape of a teenage son. I wrapped poor dead Jonathan in the rug Alex Somerfield had helped me buy in Peshawar. I found a nice irony in that, by the way."

Bogdanovic made a disgusted face.

"With the body in the inside-out carpet and tied up at both ends, plus around the middle, the super and the gorilla son and I lugged him down the four flights and into the back of my minivan. Not without the scare of my life, however. About halfway down, the bundle slipped from our grips and I had visions of Jonathan coming unwrapped. But luck was with me."

"The medical examiner said the body had been laid down and then roughly handled. But the body wasn't bruised. That was quite a head scratcher, believe me."

Bogdanovic asked, "Why did you leave him in the boathouse?"

"My intent was to bury him in the cellar."

"You told me about that cellar on Sunday," Flynn said. "You said you planned to cement it over."

"Yes. But then I mulled over the inescapable fact that the day would come when Jonathan could be missed. Maybe right away by his lover. An investigation might ensue. I decided the best thing to do was let him be found right away . . . *on my property.*"

Flynn and Bogdanovic spoke simultaneously. "Why?"

"I reasoned that after being initially suspected, I would be disregarded. What murderer parks the body on his own doorstep?"

"It worked," Flynn said. "For a while."

"Then the mystery writer in me took over the plot. In order to keep the spotlight off me, I needed somebody for the police to go chasing after, with no chance of succeeding."

Bogdanovic grunted. "Valentine. The man who never was."

"Not yet, Sergeant B. My first thought was to try to pin it on Alex. But on reflection, I rejected the idea because there'd be no guarantee that Alex would not, in self-defense, point the finger right back at me. And in the process let it be known that I'd also killed a man in Saigon a quarter of a century ago. But when I went looking for Alex on his boat on Saturday, he'd taken off on *Karla.* I had to lie in wait until he got back."

"Tell us about the knife you used," Flynn said.

"It was the one Somerfield had given me in Saigon to use on Giap. How's that for cruel irony?"

"Now about the sword stick."

"I figured I should plant some evidence that would serve to deflect police attention as to time."

"The cape and the cane indicated Dodge had gone home after the Edgars dinner."

"Exactly. Putting them there required getting that kid out of the house."

"How did you manage that?" Bogdanovic asked.

"I phoned him Saturday morning, using a very sinister and threatening voice, and told him his lover was dead and that he was going to be next. When I visited at Gramercy Park that afternoon—I had a key, as you know—I found Jimmy had taken the hint and absconded with a good deal of Jonathan's possessions. That is, the things a kid like him viewed as valuable. I left the cape and the Maltese Falcon sword stick and beat my hasty exit. A bit too hasty, apparently. I seem to have left a trace of tobacco ash on the handle. Or did you make it up, Miss Flynn? Was it a little detective trick?"

"I promise you it's there. Is it yours? Who knows?"

"It's always the little things. Trifles. Sherlock knew a thing or two, didn't he?"

Bogdanovic asked, "If you believed you'd frightened Clements off, then why. . . ?"

"Did I kill him?"

Bogdanovic nodded.

"Three guesses, and the last two don't count!"

"Despite your disguised voice he'd recognized it was you on the phone and tried to shake you down."

Griffith smiled wanly at Flynn. "How many detective novels, do you suppose, have included blackmail as a motive for murder? Yet the little fool tried it. I bet he never read a thriller in his life. He's the movie generation. Rock 'n' roll videos on the tube. He agreed to meet me late at night on the pier where his body was found in the water. He actually and truly believed I was going to give him one hundred thousand dollars! The poor jerk knew nothing about the book trade. Maybe Elmore Leonard would have a hundred grand. Or Mary Higgins Clark. Dick Francis, yes! But Morgan Griffith?"

"The knife?"

"An old Army bayonet. I tossed it in the river."

As a silence settled in the room, Flynn heard chirping birds a long way off. She rose from the floor and settled in the chair.

"Well, is that all of it?" Bogdanovic demanded.

Griffith ignored him and kept his eyes on Flynn. "The mystery writer in me needs to know what was your first clue. The finger smudge on the cane?"

She looked down. "The carpet."

"Really? You had no idea until today?"

"It caught my attention on Sunday. But I had no idea I was looking at a clue. It just struck me as odd that one of the first things you moved into your new house was an obviously expensive Oriental rug. If I owned a rug like this, I would not want moving men tramping all over it with dirty shoes. I don't know any woman who would."

"Amazing! That never occurred to me."

"Then I found out about the multicolored fibers on Dodge's tuxedo. But even then the carpet did not fully register. Maybe, subconsciously, I didn't want it to. You see, I like you, Morgan. I liked you right off the bat when we were walking up that muddy hillside from the boathouse. I like writers."

"I'm touched, Arlene. Truly I am. For what it's worth, I liked you right away, too. I still do. I like detectives."

"As to the carpet, when I saw it today, the possibility of its being the source of the fibers finally clicked. I decided I'd better have a closer look."

"So you sent Sergeant B down the hill to ruin his two-hundred-dollar shoes."

"When I flipped a corner of the carpet back to examine the knotting, I found the caked mud. My first impression was that a corner of it had been dragged. But when I rolled it up a little more there was too much mud for that to be the explanation. I pictured you dragging the carpet down the hill with Dodge's body wrapped in it."

"I didn't drag. I laid it down and rolled it."

"Who is Gene Valentine?"

"Nobody. I made up the name."

"And the man with the cigarette in the picture?"

"A splendid war correspondent by the name of Craig Spence, deceased, alas. Friend of Jonathan's. Died of AIDS while I was in Peshawar buying that carpet. Was that all you had? The rug on my floor and the ash smudge on Jonathan's Maltese Falcon cane?"

"There are lots of bits and pieces that make more sense now than they did before. You knew the title of Somerfield's book but said you had not read it. You also referred to it as a *roman à clef*. Obviously, you had read it."

"I was, in fact, reading the disc on my word processor at the very moment Fulmer came barging in all upset about someone being dead in the boathouse."

"What did you think of the book?"

"Not one of Alex's best. Were those all your clues?"

"You said you never heard a boat on the river but you told me you'd heard a dog barking down by the water on the night you were shot at. That is, the night you staged the shooting."

"I was afraid that would seem a touch too melodramatic."

"I believed you."

"Or, perhaps, wanted to? Subconsciously?"

She shrugged.

"Now you see what Holmes meant about emotions interfering with the logical faculties."

She stood and walked to the fireplace. "May I back you up for a moment to clarify something?"

"I'm your prisoner. I have waived all Miranda rights against self-incrimination. I'm glad it's over with."

"If you killed the man in Vietnam as part of an American intelligence operation, why were you so concerned that nobody know about it? It was years ago. We were at war. You were recruited for the act by an American agent operating on the orders of the U.S. government."

He nodded slowly. "All true."

"Then why be worried the story might get out now? Ex-agents and former spies are spilling the beans all over the place, with no repercussions. Some are making big bucks in books and movies."

"Because I wasn't carrying out Somerfield's orders."

"Excuse me? The killing of Giap was personal?"

"It was official. But not for Somerfield's CIA. That he recruited me was a fluke. I happened to be working for someone else who wanted Giap dead."

"The South Vietnamese government?"

"If they knew about Giap, I'm sure they would have wanted him dead, as well. You see, Giap was a double agent."

"He was working for both the United States and the North Vietnamese?"

"He was an agent for the United States and the Soviet Union. It was Moscow that ordered me to hit him."

Bogdanovic blared, "Hold it a second. *Moscow?*"

"What Somerfield did not know, and what I could never let him know, was that I was KGB. I'd been recruited by them in college. I got the rank of major—I was the youngest KGB major ever, at twenty-two. I retired with the rank of colonel in 1989, just a few days before the Berlin Wall came down. But I'd been inactivated well before that. The irony in this—well, one of the ironies—is that I thought I'd have to kill Jonathan years ago. I was terrified he'd unmask me while he was researching his book on Soviet espionage."

"Secrets of Lubyanka," Flynn said.

"A very naive book. I don't know if he discovered my secret. Maybe he did and decided to keep it to himself."

"Why should he do that?"

"I was his friend. The only one, actually."

42

Next Case

CHIEF OF DETECTIVES Harvey Goldstein sat tilted back in his chair with his head cradled in his hands and amazingly small feet parked on the desk.

Bogdanovic had folded himself into his customary chair.

Flynn stood at the window, the morning light turning her into a slim silhouette cutout. In summarizing the case she had spoken for fifteen minutes.

Three days had gone by since she formally placed Morgan Griffith under arrest.

Another few minutes passed silently before Goldstein dismantled his hands and swung his feet off the desk. "Where is he at the moment?"

Flynn came away from the window and settled in her chair. "The Feds are questioning him. That should take quite a while. They've got forty years of espionage to talk about. He started working for the Russians in 1955. That's practically the whole damn history of the Cold War."

Bogdanovic shifted in the deep chair. "They ought to save their breath and shoot the crummy traitor."

"Speaking of shooting," Goldstein said, shuffling through a stack of papers on the desk, "I received a reply this morning to a query I sent out day before yesterday to Interpol. I asked if they could find out from the Vietnamese police what was the final disposition of that Tu Do Street homicide. It was so long ago, I figured nobody would know. Or even care. But I was mistaken. The Vietnamese interior ministry reported that an arrest was made in 1972, three years after the murder."

"Oh God no," Flynn gasped.

"The accused was one of the pimps who worked that street and shunted customers into the bar that was run by this man Giap, who arranged for the women. Police say there'd been a falling out between the two men. But it took those three years for a detective to crack the case. The man he arrested was promptly tried, convicted, and executed by a military firing squad."

Flynn shook her head. "I wonder if Griffith knows he's got a fifth death on his conscience."

"If he has one," Bogdanovic said. "Which I doubt."

"Did you ever ask him why he did it?" Goldstein asked.

"Was there a scene in the detention cell like the one George Smiley and Bill Haydon had in *Tinker, Tailor, Soldier, Spy?* Yes, but there was no deep philosophical discourse. No angry polemics on his part. He wasn't an ideologue. He had no deep-rooted anger. No indirect getting back at someone for some slight or abuse. He spouted none of the socioeconomic-political mumbo-jumbo that was the hallmark of domestic protestors of the Vietnam War period. No moral outrage. No anti-nuclear fervor. He was a typical example of the buttoned-down, buttoned-up kids of the Eisenhower years."

"Then what was his reason?"

"At first it was his curiosity. The idea of leading a double life. I think he eventually came to like the money, although he never admitted to avarice. Then it became the sheer thrill of doing something and getting away with it that the rest of us mere mortals could only know vicariously by watching a television show about spies or going to the movies. Or in our reading. I'm not a psychologist, but I came away sensing Griffith had always seen himself as the main character in a book."

"A real sick mind," Bogdanovic muttered.

"One thing that intrigued me that I asked him about," Flynn continued, "was why he suddenly decided, after living so long in the city, to buy the old Ilona Troy estate. He looked at me as if I were the most stupid person ever to walk the planet, then said it was the name of the place."

Bogdanovic snorted. "Traitor's Lair. What an unbelievable display of arrogance!"

"Or was it a subconscious, maybe even conscious, confession? His way of admitting a sin without having to do penance."

Another leaden silence settled around them.

Stirring at last, Goldstein asked, "What's on Arlene Flynn's immediate docket?"

"I'll do what I can to bolster my boss's brief for holding Griffith's trial in Stone County. The Manhattan D.A. is staking out his claim to the honor. Benson is worried that the Feds will try to elbow them both aside to try Griffith for treason. Since he was a spy during wartime, he could get the death penalty."

"Good," said Bogdanovic.

"After you dispose of this case, what?" Goldstein asked.

"The boss has handed me a new one that looks interesting. Two nights ago an elderly man and his wife were found beaten to death in their home. It looked at first blush to the town police to be a routine break-in robbery that went awry."

Goldstein smiled. "But?"

"There are indications they might have been set up by their ne'er-do-well dope-using daughter. She claims an ironclad alibi. However, I think I've spotted a teeny crack in it."

Slowly rocking, Goldstein said, "If the day dawns when you think you'd like a change of scenery, the welcome mat is always out for you at my cop shop."

She shifted her eyes to Bogdanovic. "I'd say you're in excellent shape on the personnel side, Chief."

"Sergeant Bogdanovic? Yeah, Johnny's definitely got promise. But I'd feel a hell of a lot better about him if I could get him to crack open a good mystery novel every now and then. With you around I'd have someone literate to talk to."

She reached between their chairs and touched Bogdanovic's hand. "In the time-honored tradition of the final scene in all good detective stories," she said, "there's one thing about this case that puzzles me, Johnny."

"Is that so? What?"

"How *did* you persuade Elvira Eveland to just hand over the Somerfield manuscript?"

He lifted himself out of his slouch. "There was nothing to it. I called her up and told her I was thinking of trying my hand at writing a mystery, but that I wasn't sure I had the right stuff and could she spare me some time to sit down and talk about it."

"Naturally, she invited you to lunch."

He grinned. "Then it was just a function of the overwhelming power of the Bogdanovic charm."

"Ah! You got the old gal soused."

Bogdanovic winked. "Exactly!"